THE WHOLE STORY

SUZI WIELAND

Copyright ©2018 by Suzi Wieland
All rights reserved. The reproduction or utilization of this work in whole or in part, by any means, is forbidden without written permission from the author.
This book is a work of fiction. Names, characters, places, and incidents are products of the author's imagination or are used fictitiously. Any resemblance to actual events, locations, or persons, living or dead is entirely coincidental.
Published by Twisted Path Press
Cover by Krafigs Design
First edition April 2018, Second edition May 2022, Third edition July 2024

Chapter One
Basil

I raise my shot glass of whiskey into the air. "To Tuesday!" I yell.

"To Tuesday!" Denis and my other friends shout.

"Basil, honey." The waitress leans close to my ear, so close I can see down her dress, a smidgen of her black brassiere. "It's Wednesday."

"To Wednesday," I say, and the others chorus back. The buzz from the crowd at The Spot is so loud that nobody even notices our noise, almost every single table and chair filled with people who need a break from life.

The waitress gives us that knowing smile 'cause she knows her tip will be plenty, just like it is ev-ver-ry night. I go to say thank you to her—what's her name anyway?—but she's squeezing between overflowing tables and booths. I should know her name since Denis took her home a few months ago. Or was it Karl? I can't remember. All I know is that she's a sweet girl.

THE WHOLE STORY

Denis pokes me in the shoulder. "Hey, I got something to celebrate on my last week of freedom. Come with me to the bar so the snoopy boys won't see."

I follow him away from our friends, my worn shoes sticking the floor. Starting next week, Denis is going to work for a bricklayer. I wish I could be working alongside him, but Mumsy won't let me get a job. It's pathetic, I know, but it's the truth.

We sidle up to the bar, and the frazzled bartender takes our order, grabbing a few of the empty glasses sitting there. After he hustles away, Denis pulls his grimy hand out of his pocket to show me four brown beans. "Einar called them papu. Said they'd make our night more interesting."

I finger the oval beans and sniff. Nothing. "They're beans. I think Einar ripped you off."

Denis gets this smirk all over his face. "No, they're pills. He assured me they were the newest thing."

Normally me and my buddies stay away from this type of stuff. We know what happens to the stupid dunderheads addicted to drugs, but this is different. Next week my best buddy will be working twelve-hour days. He'll probably get all mature and responsible, make some coin, which will find him a decent girl. Then he'll want to settle down and forget about us other losers. And I'll still be stuck in my dreary life taking care of my sick mother, stuck in the same hole for the rest of my life. Without my best friend.

Denis would probably smack me if he knew what I'm thinking. This guy has been with me through the roughest parts of my life. He won't let me slip away so easily.

"What the hell." I pop the two pills into my mouth. I'm ready for more fun.

"What are you two boys doing over here? You know I can get you your drinks." The waitress stands between us, her arms draped over our shoulders, somehow smelling sweet even though she's been working hours in this stanky bar. She's holding on to both of us, but her red nails kinda walk across Denis' shoulder.

Yeah, it was definitely Denis that banged her.

"Didn't want to work you too hard." Denis grins, and she returns it. I got a feeling she's forgotten all about me. "What time you get done?"

"Midnight. Will you still be around?"

"You know I will." Her demure smile almost makes me laugh. She's a wild one, if I remember what Denis told me last.

They finish their moony eyes at each other, and we make it back to our seats. I hope those pills kick in 'cause right now I've got no lady prospects of my own.

But the night is still young.

THE WHOLE STORY

I stumble down the dark, dusty road towards my house. The only light comes from the stars since most people are in bed now. I'm always the last one to get home 'cause I live on the far edge of town. Nobody past us except for the cows and trees. Luckily there aren't barely any wagons out this time of night 'cause I don't want to get run over by them horses. Still have to watch out for those piles of dung though.

The houses out here are set far apart, if you can call them houses. Shacks mostly, including ours. But we got huge yards and trees to provide privacy, about the only thing good about living out here. A few of my buddies live in those cramped apartments in town, but I prefer living on the edge of town.

The latch to the front gate is still broken, and I swing the door wide open. The dirt path to my front door curves back and forth, but I manage to stay on it. The dang thing was straight this morning though. My stomach pitches—sweet mother almighty—must be all that potato pie I ate earlier.

I'll have to be careful when I climb the ladder to my bed. My only personal space is my loft, a small sleeping area above Mumsy's bedroom. It gets a little hot, and it's noisy when the rain pounds on the tin roof just above me, and I've only got room to sit up, but at least it's my own spot.

Mumsy is slouching down on the couch, her bottle of wine sitting empty on the floor. Some dried food that wasn't there earlier coats the armrest, shiny and wet like jelly. I hope it won't stain the couch.

But who am I kidding? It'll just join one of the many other stains Mumsy has added.

"You're late," she snips, that stupid book folded across her lap. We both know she's been reading that same bloody book for years. "You'd better not have tracked horse dung into the house."

"I didn't." The stench of her unwashed skin and the stifling air fills my nose. I'll have to help her with her bath tomorrow, one of the chores I hate. I step over her cane and head across the only other room in our two-room house. I'd open a window, but she's probably going to her bedroom now.

"You'd better be up before noon." Her shrill voice drills into my head.

I rarely sleep in until noon. "I'll have breakfast ready at eight." She usually wakes by then and goes back to sleep after her belly is full.

"Where you going?" she asks as I hit the door to the backyard. "You're taking me to the market tomorrow. You didn't take me yesterday."

THE WHOLE STORY

"Of course." My head is pounding too, and I'd get another drink to take care of it, but the squall in my stomach is growing. I can't get sick in the house. Mumsy will screech at me for an hour.

I get the door closed and escape into the backyard, my stomach screaming. My knees hit the ground, and I can't hold back the eruption inside me. I spew all over the grass, again and again, until finally nothing is left. I roll away from the stench and lie on my back staring at the twinkling lights in the sky. A thistle brushes against my ear, and I move away from it.

With no street lights and less homes on the edge of town, we can see so many stars. My old girl Melina used to like sitting out here staring up, pointing out the pictures in the sky. What did she call them? Constellations, I think. I used to sneak her back here after Mumsy went to sleep, and we'd get busy under those bright stars. She was a nice girl… a decent girl… but she couldn't put up with Mumsy's constant criticisms and demands.

I couldn't blame her for dumping me.

A lady-friend would be nice about now, but I wasn't so lucky like Denis. He'll make fun of me tomorrow when he hears about my puking episode. I stare at the rancid pool of vomit on the brown grass. I hadn't drank any more tonight than any other night, and I rarely throw up.

Denis lied. Those things he gave me, the papu, they didn't work for either of us. Maybe that's what made me sick. If you can't trust your best friend to give you good drugs, who can you trust?

Course Einar probably bamboozled Denis, made him believe the pills were good. I hope Denis didn't pay too much for them.

I need to rinse my mouth out with water, maybe dump some over my head, but I have no energy to crawl over to the well, so I remain still. The ground is so hard, the grass scratchy, but my eyes are heavy. I'll rest for a minute and then go inside to my cramped loft.

Chapter Two
Nissa

"Nissa," Mother calls from the kitchen where she's been baking a ton of sugar cookies all morning. I've been waiting to raid her cookie stash.

"Yes?" I pop my head into the room. "You must need a cookie tester." I glance over at my little sister. Giselle is leaning against the cookie-covered counter, waiting with the patience of a typical eight-year-old. Flower smudges her bright green skirt and matching polka dot shirt. "I have more cookie experience than Giselle after all."

"Hey." Giselle's hands fly to her hips, and she scowls at me. "I've been helping Mother. Not you."

Her headband slips forward, and she pushes it back, holding her brown braids in place. She's too cute with her adorable chubby face and the flour and grease-covered formerly white apron.

"Okay." I shrug as if it's no big deal.

SUZI WIELAND

I pad over to Giselle and climb on my ladder-stool so I can reach the counter. I'm fourteen years older than her but am six inches shorter. I lost the gene lottery, was born a mini-g, a giant who's more the size of a normie than the giants of my world.

At least on my special stool, I'm taller than her now.

"You shouldn't get any since you didn't help us." Giselle plays up the tough girl act, but she'll be offering me cookies as soon as Mother gives her the okay.

"But I'm taking you on the camping trip," I throw back at her. Mother's ten dozen cookies are for the HoneyBee bake sale, the money being raised to take the girls on a camping trip to Milandia Park. I volunteered to be a chaperone: ten eight-year-olds, two mums, and me tenting it in the park for two nights.

I'd only do it for my sister and her group. I know the parents and Honeybees, and they treat me with respect, unlike other kids her age who don't know me. I'm shorter than them, so they act as if *I'm* the child.

"We figured out the tent. It'll be Margrete and Viola. Then me. Then you. Mrs. Iverson said we'll have someone else with us, but I don't know who yet. Viola wants it to be Fria, but I really don't care. Well, I don't want it to be Bergit. She hasn't been very nice to Margrete lately." Giselle finally takes a breath.

THE WHOLE STORY

Mother and I exchange glances, and she brings a bowl over to the sink.

"Did you get all that?" she asks with a laugh as she rinses the white flour off her dark skin.

"I think so."

She points to the cupboard. "I hate to interrupt the camping talk, but I discovered I'm low on sugar. I'll never make it through the next two batches. Will you and Giselle run to the market to get some?"

I scan the plastic container on the counter, at least a quarter full of sugar. Plenty.

Giselle claps her hands together, her eyes bright. "Can we go to Moorgan, Mother? Nissa was talking about the market there and all the neat things. Can we, please?"

"Moorgan?"

Instead of a twenty-minute trip to the market, it's become an afternoon visit to the normies' world down below us. Not that I mind. I've been working there for a few months, and it'll soon be my home.

Mother puts on her contemplative face, and I hide my smile, pretty sure she wanted Giselle out of the kitchen for a while. "I guess so. You can take a few cookies with too."

"I'm not going until you clean up." I point to the flower on her shirt.

SUZI WIELAND

She untucks the shirt and waves it back and forth, sending the flower particles into the air. "I'm ready." She grins.

Mother and I exchange a laugh.

I slide off my stool so we're side-by-side now. I've never felt normal next to my nine-and-a-half-foot mum and my eleven-foot pop, but Giselle is closer to my size… for now. It won't be long, and she'll be towering over me too.

"Okay, let's go, squirt," I tell her. She wrinkles her nose at me, but she loves her nickname.

At six feet, Giselle's height is normal for an eight-year-old giant, but she's got that baby face still, so no normie would mistake her for being older than me.

Mother gives us the coins, and Giselle takes off for her room to get her own money for a treat, even though we've got four cookies in a bag.

Soon we're heading down the sidewalk on our way to Lyft No. 2, which is eight blocks away from our home. Giselle skips along on the green grass beside me, humming her favorite song. I'll miss Kjempeland when I move, the thick leafy trees and lush lawns, and the vibrant colors of the giants' homes. Moorgan has trees of course, but not as many, and the normie houses are smushed into smaller spaces. Or they live in apartments in the city. Their homes and buildings are bland browns

THE WHOLE STORY

and whites, with little variation. One day when I can afford my own home, I'll paint it bright blue like my parents' house.

A wagon rolls past us in the street, the rancid smell of horse poop enveloping me. All horses in the streets wear the bun bags to catch their manure, but that's not the case in Moorgan. I'll have to point that out to Giselle if I see a horse pooping in the street down below.

Giselle.

Her humming is gone. I turn around and scan the sidewalk behind me, unable to see her peach dress. I open my mouth, about to call her name, but spot her kneeling on the grass talking to Mrs. Patacki and cradling their new puppy.

"She's adorable, Mrs. Patacki. How's it going?" I reach down and pet the squirming thing on its head. "Is it a German Shepherd?"

"Yes. The potty training isn't fun, and he cries at night still, but it'll get better."

"I want a puppy." Giselle snuggles the dog to her cheek.

"I know," I say, "but you know that Father is allergic to them. Otherwise we'd probably have one."

"You can come visit mine any time you want." Mrs. Patacki pats Giselle on her back and stands. She's over nine feet tall, like most other women, and although nobody treats me badly for being so short, it's hard not to feel different.

My parents have tried to make me feel as normal as everybody else, but when you have to get your clothes from the normie world, everybody knows they're different. Or when you have tiny furniture in your bedroom compared to your friends, you can't help but compare yourself to them, seeing only the differences and not the similarities.

With only maybe six mini-g's in our town of five thousand, I'm a bit of an oddity.

"We'd better get going. Why don't you say goodbye to Mrs. Patacki."

Giselle says her goodbyes and sets the puppy down, then jumps to her feet. "I'm ready for my four cookies now."

"Four?" I say as I lead her away. We stop to cross the gravel street, waiting for the wagon to pass, and Giselle waves to the horses. They're bred to be slightly larger than the horses in Moorgan, stockier especially, but otherwise are the same.

"Well, yeah. I figured you'd share yours with me."

"But then that leaves me with none."

"Okay," she sighs as if she's sacrificing something important. "You can have one."

"Thanks." I laugh at the drama of my silly girl.

THE WHOLE STORY

The wagon traffic gets heavier closer to the lyft. Giselle wipes the cookie crumbs off her mouth as I pay for our two tickets to go down to Moorgan.

Kjempeland has several lyfts, each attached to beanstalks. Two cars are constantly going up and down each lyft, carrying passengers. It's not busy right now, and we don't have to wait long with the group of mostly men in overalls and boots, who work on farms or in large factories where they don't hit their heads on the ceilings.

Most of the people on the lyft are adults, and I'm literally half the size of some of them, the taller men at least. I step into the corner, the safest spot for me. I've gotten my feet stepped on enough times by giants who weren't paying attention.

Giselle stands by the window to watch on the ride down, which will only take five minutes. Kjempeland and the other giant cities are over a mile above the ground, and although normies and giants often mix, we usually stick to our own cities. It's impossible for a giant to live among the same buildings and houses in Moorgan, and it's difficult for normies to live in our world. Everything is just too big.

My parents provided me with smaller everything, stools, and ladders and other necessities from the normie world, but not every mini-g is as lucky as me.

The car rumbles to life, and we descend through the ground. It's dark for a short time, but then we emerge into the blue sky and clouds above Moorgan. The way the car winds down the stalk gives a three hundred sixty degree view, and Giselle's eyes are glued to the town spreading out below. Moorgan is about triple the size of Kjempeland, and it's a wondrous sight to see from above.

"Their buildings are so close together." Her mouth gapes at the world below her, and I stifle my laugh.

"They don't appreciate the green space as much as us. Instead of their own yards, they have spacious parks that everyone can use." Giants don't have apartment buildings, and I figured it'd be easier to let her see it instead of trying to explain it. "Some houses do have their own yards though, especially in the wealthier neighborhoods."

"I'd be sad without a yard."

"Me too." My apartment has a small green space, but I'll miss being able to walk out a door into a yard, miss having fires on cool nights, miss playing yard games with my family.

Moorgan is also different from Kjempeland in other ways. We have wealthy giants who live in immense houses, but most of the giant population live fairly well.

THE WHOLE STORY

We don't have the poverty and the disparity of wealth that the normies down below have.

Giselle spins around. "I decided I want to get a treat instead of a toy."

"But you had cookies." And probably a snack before that at home. My father likes to joke that my eating habits are why they keep me around: he appreciates the lower food bills. But it's true. Giselle has been eating more than me for years now.

"I know, but the normie food looks so good. Will you get the recipes to make at home?" She's never actually seen the normie food, but I've talked about it a lot with her.

"Of course. But I'm sure you'll try a lot of it when you visit me." A pang of regret hits. In a few days I'll be leaving to move to Moorgan, and I won't get to see my sister's smiley face every day. At least the trip up the lyfts is not hard.

Giselle chats on about the normie foods, and soon the car clunks to a stop at the bottom. Only a few normies are waiting to get on the lyft to go up.

We step out and head down the sidewalk. Giselle stares up at the four-story brick apartment buildings in awe, her gaze running along the ten or more windows in a row. "Is this what your place looks like? It's like they're all living in a big box together."

SUZI WIELAND

The buildings downtown are a bit stifling, building after building with no space between them.

"It's not so bad inside, and my building has a grassy yard I can use." I'd love one of those apartments with a balcony, but my budget doesn't allow something like that right now.

The streets are busy, and her head whips around to take in the sights and smells. The carriages and wagons bumping down the roads are so much smaller than ours, and Giselle doesn't even notice the strange look she gets from the people we're passing. We seem like twins from behind, with our brown hair and dark skin, but from the front, her face and chubby cheeks tell a different story. Well, and our clothes. Giselle's shorter skirt shows off her knobby, dirty knees, but I'm in a more proper-lengthed skirt like both giant and normie women wear.

We pass a restaurant with a crowd of people standing out front. Giselle takes a deep breath, her eyes widening. "I'm so short. I mean they're short. Or I'm normal."

"No kidding." She finally understands how I feel. In Moorgan, I can easily look many people in the eye when I speak with them. I can wash my hands at the sink without having to use a stepstool. I can walk into a store and find clothes that fit me.

THE WHOLE STORY

I lead her to a park and let her play for a while, and we soon arrive at the market. Rows and rows of tented booths fill the cram-packed market. Tables of fruit and vegetables, fresh-baked breads and pastries, racks of clothing, home goods, and other trinkets. The scents of spices and food overwhelm the smell of normies sweat, and I take a deep breath.

The sugar is the first thing I get, and then we can explore. Giselle goes on the hunt, for what I'm not sure, but it'll probably be brightly colored or make noise if she doesn't get any food. We wander around from tent to tent for a while, with me following her.

She bypasses the clothing and makes note of which food booths she wants to return to. As she searches through the trinkets on the table, I check out the guy across the aisle from me. He covers a yawn and glances around the market. He's following an older woman, maybe his mother, with a basket of food in his arms, but then looks up at me and smiles.

"What about this one?" He holds up a shiny red pepper from the wood crate for his mother to inspect, swiping his curly blond hair out of his eyes.

She scowls at the poor vegetable. "No, that one is bruised." She sets it down and picks through the others one by one. Eventually her hand circles back to the original one, and she studies it again. "This is the only decent one in the bunch." She sighs and places it in the basket.

"I know, Mumsy." He glances over at me and smirks, his adorable blue eyes twinkling. Must be those long lashes that make them stand out. "Did you need any tomatoes?"

"Of course we do." She huffs and moves on to the tomato section, complaining about how the quality of these fruits and vegetables have gone down. The poor guy nods and mumbles along.

I make my way over to the bin and pick one up. The plump, heavy tomato smells sweet and earthy. Perfect.

"This one is ready." I offer it to the guy because, despite everything his mother is saying about the tomatoes, she obviously has no idea how to find a good one.

"Thank you." He takes the tomato from me, his fingertips brushing my hand. His gaze stays on me for a few seconds too long, and my cheeks warm.

"Mumsy, here's a better one." He shows her my pick, and she sets down the one with the green patch on the skin.

I take a deep breath—this guy smells so good, like being in a forest of pine trees.

"This one is too red, Basil." His mother glares at the tomato as if it's done something wrong.

THE WHOLE STORY

"Too red?" He throws me an is-she-crazy? look. I laugh quietly as she goes back to scrutinizing the tomatoes again.

A flash catches my eyes. Giselle is two booths down already, and I take a step away, but the guy grabs my arm. "Thanks for your help, um…'"

"Nissa," I say, my face burning. "I'm sorry. I need to catch my sister."

Giselle hits the corner and disappears, so I take off after her. She's on a mission, but if she realizes I'm not with her, she might panic. She doesn't know her way around here yet.

A girl about five runs straight into me and bounces to the ground. She peers up at me stunned, but then a smile graces her face. I apologize and help her up.

Over her shoulder, I see Basil—that's what his mother called him—staring at me, and I give him the thumbs up. He does it back and then turns towards his mother.

"Leese, you need to watch where you're going." A mother rushes over and grips her arm, a contrite look on her face. "Sorry, miss."

"I think we're both okay." I'm used to little girls not paying attention.

The girl nods.

SUZI WIELAND

Giselle pops back into view now, and I relax. Basil is still watching me, and the butterflies flutter in my stomach. I know he's just grateful for my help, sharing a moment about his picky mother, but I can't help think about what dating might be like down here. Men who are my size. My only worry is if they'll care that I'm a giant. A lot of people have no issues with giants down here, but there are some who don't want our kind around.

It's silly really. Dating is not anything I have time for right now. I've got my job and new apartment, not to mention all the trips back up the lyft I'll be taking to Kjempeland. No, dating should not be my focus.

Maybe soon though.

Chapter Three
Basil

"How about that one?" Denis motions to another cutie at the bar. All night long, he's been pointing out girls for me, but I can only think about that fox at the market.

Nissa. That's her name. I haven't seen her around, but why would I? From the look of her clothes and soft hands, I'm guessing she's got a classier set of friends than mine.

"Naw." It was stinking stupid, but when she was standing next to me, handing me that tomato, all I wanted to do was reach out and touch those long braids that covered her head. They were weird, but cool weird, like a rope almost, the way the strands twisted around, but they were shiny and sleek.

Denis says something else, but I'm picturing Nissa's jugs.

"What's your deal tonight?" Denis pokes me in the forehead, and I whack his hand.

"Nothing." Just bored of the usual girls.

"Must be a big nothing, because I said we should head back to my house soon."

"Sorry." I shrug. If I tell him I'm picturing some girl's jugs, he'll probably forgive me. "You think they're gone?" His parents are leaving for two days, which mean their house is available for a party pad. Maybe some fun at Denis' will get my mind off that Nissa girl. "We'd better start spreading the word."

Denis didn't want to tell anyone until his parents were safely gone. He'd had people show up at his house for a party before, got busted 'cause his parents were still home.

"Not yet. I changed my mind, so the party will be tomorrow. I've got other plans for tonight. You in?" He motions with his head to look off to the side. Two giggly girls sit at a table, their short dresses barely covering their knees. The blonde one tilts her head and slides a sexy smile my way. "You can have the blonde one," he says.

He always gives me the blonde one 'cause of my stupid blond curls. I like black-haired girls, and brunettes, and redheads. I fancy them all.

The girl he wants is playing with the chain around her neck that disappears between her jugs. The women here are just like us: they want to escape their crappy lives for a short time. They'll get drunk with us, we'll bang them, and then they'll go home. They don't give a damn

THE WHOLE STORY

about who we are, just like we don't give a damn about them.

Not like Nissa today at the market. She probably wouldn't go back to a complete stranger's house to have sex. She's a good girl. I can tell by the way she was worried about her sister, by the way she blushed and looked away when I stared too long. Yeah, I really don't know her, but it's a feeling I got.

The expression on Nissa's face when her sister slammed into her makes me chuckle again. Luckily she walked off unscathed.

I check out the two girls again. The blonde is cute, but she's not Nissa. But Nissa isn't here, and even if she was, she'd never stoop to dating someone like me.

"I'm in," I say. "I suppose we have to buy them a drink." Funds are low right now. They're always low.

Denis laughs. "A night in the sack with her is worth it."

"You're right." I have to kick Nissa out of my mind. "Let's get on it."

I might not see Nissa again, but I can see her in my mind any time I want, and even though I'll be bedding that other girl, Nissa will be in my head.

I stack the last bit of wood behind the house, wipe my forehead, which is wet more from the humidity than my work, and lean the axe against the wall. I probably should've gone inside and told Mumsy I'm home from Denis', but I needed to get the wood cut before I start on my other chores.

I used to spend a lot more time at Denis' house than I do now. Before her accident, Mumsy worked a lot of night shifts, and I usually stayed at his house whenever she was gone. Adding one more kid to a gaggle of eight doesn't really make much of a difference. I always loved staying at his house because he got his water from the sink instead of a well. It was always cold, and easier than bringing up water from the well.

I head into the house and cover my nose at the putrid smell. Mumsy has the ability to go outside to the privy, but she always uses a chamber pot instead. I quickly dispose of her waste and return the bowl. I'd tried getting rid of it completely a while back, but she used whatever was available.

The smell lingers, and I open the window, hoping the breeze will clean the air.

"Basil!" Mumsy screeches.

"I'm coming." I wish she could still work, but after she got injured on the job a few years back, she's been unable to do much. I'd give anything to get out of the

THE WHOLE STORY

house to work myself, but other than doing a few odd jobs for the neighbors when she isn't paying attention, I can't get away. I used to work, started at fourteen, but Mumsy's injury four years later derailed our lives. If only she'd let me work, then she could find better doctors who could make her better.

Luckily, we have enough to live off with her alms from the sisters, supplemented with a random win here or there when I play dice on the streets. It isn't a pretty life, but we're surviving.

I kick her clothes out of my path. She blames her injuries for everything, but she's lazier than everyone I know. This and the garbage all around is why I barely ever bring anyone home.

I stick my head into her tiny bedroom. The only thing there, the only thing there's room for, is a dresser with a missing drawer and her bed. "I just finished chopping another load of wood for the stove." I open the window in her room to rid it of the smell of rotting food and dirty clothes.

"Did you get my coin yet?" She glares at me from her bed, her stained nightgown drooping too low. I turn my head, not wanting to see her limp, flabby jugs.

"No. I'll go do that now." I can get over there before it's time to eat, and then I'll start the laundry after lunch, depending on the coming rain. Our shack isn't big enough to hang many clothes.

"No, I'm getting hungry. And why weren't you up this morning getting it? You know how important that coin is. If you'd go out and get a job, we wouldn't have to live in this dump-hole."

This.

Again.

"You're right, Mumsy. I was talking to Denis, and he heard they had openings at the factory."

"No, you will not work at the factory," she spit, a fire in her eyes. "Who's going to feed me when you're gone for ten hours a day? Who's going to help me to the privy and give me my medicine? I know how it works with some stranger who cares for the sick and elderly. They'll probably try and poison me when you're gone. Then they'll steal my coin and my pills."

What coin? I almost scoff. The coin from the sisters is a pittance.

"I told Denis that job won't work anyway. I'll go get your alms now." I back out of the doorway. This same scene plays out any time I talk about finding work. About the only jobs I qualify for are ones with ten-hour days or longer, which I'd take in a heartbeat, but she's too scared to be alone that long.

THE WHOLE STORY

"And tell your friends not to show up here so early?"

I was with Denis, and the other guys knew I was at his place. Besides, they don't come around here 'cause they don't like dealing with Mumsy.

"Who are you talking about?"

"Some hussy."

Oh no. Nissa. Did she find me somehow? I can't bear to think about her seeing our squalid home. I'll never live it down. But no, it can't be Nissa. There's no reason she'd come searching for me anyway, just because we spoke at the market.

"Who, Mumsy?"

"It's not like I could write her name down after I had to drag myself out of bed to get the door. At ten this morning." Mumsy glares at me. "She had blonde hair and said she was with you last night. Is that why you weren't home? You were bonking some floozy?"

"Eva?" Not sure why she'd show up here. I made it clear that last night was a one-time thing.

"Eva." Mumsy huffs. "That's right. You tell that girl not to come so early next time."

There won't be a next time.

"She said she'll be back later. I had to tell her I had no idea where my son was. How do you think that felt?

My son, who's supposed to be caring for me? It's ridiculous, Basil. I won't stand for—"

I shut the bedroom door and lean against it, ignoring my yelling mother. There's no good reason why Eva should've come here. Yeah, the sex was good, but we had nothing in common, and I didn't get the impression that she liked me much either.

Maybe if I invite her over, Mumsy will scare her away. It's worked before.

"I'll make dinner," I call and hustle away. An empty bag sits on the counter and a greasy pan on the stove. I sniff the air, noticing the slight scent of something burnt. I open the garbage, and the full smell hits me. Several thick pieces of charred bread and cheese lays on the top.

All the energy drains out of me. That loaf was supposed to last us a few more days, and there's barely a few bites out of the scrunched up pieces. One more thing I need to add to my list. I have too much to do.

Laundry.

Covering that rusty hole in the roof with another piece of tin before it starts leaking water.

Making more soap with the lye I purchased yesterday.

Stitching the hole in my shirt before it grows too big, and then I'm down to only three shirts.

THE WHOLE STORY

Plus all the other things I have to do. When I go get her alms, I'm stopping by the alehouse for a quick drink. I deserve it.

Mumsy is seated at the table when I get home, her hands gripping the glass that's probably filled with cheap wine. I want to sneak up to my loft and hide, but I have to face the piper. I shouldn't have gone down to the District, but I'd done so well there last time. I was even winning my first few games of dice. I should've walked away then, but I didn't, and now I'd lost a bit of Mumsy's alms.

"Where have you been?" she snaps. "Bring my coin over here."

"I'm going to put it in the bank." I head towards the dinky box where we keep our coin.

"No. Bring it here." She eyes my clothes. "And don't get the floor all wet." As if I'm dripping everywhere. My clothes are barely damp from the light shower.

I trudge over and dig in my pants. The coin goes on the table, and she counts it. She purses her lips and glares up at me. "Where's the rest?"

There's no use in lying. "I stopped down at the District. I was doing good until—"

SUZI WIELAND

She pelts me in the face with the coins. "Didn't I warn you not to go there? This is my coin, Basil. My coin. And how are we supposed to live when you threw away half of it?"

"It's not half. Not even a quarter." I was just trying to make more for us… for her. It's not my fault I lost.

Her wrinkly faces goes red and puffy. "I'm tired of you stealing my coin. You'd better get it back." She whacks her cane on the floor, and I jump.

How am I supposed to do that? She won't give me more coin, so I won't be able to go to the District again and win it back. She won't let me get a job.

"You'd better get it, or I'm going to call the sheriff and tell them you stole it. Now get out of my face." She pokes me hard in the chest with the cane, and I stumble backwards. At least it won't leave a bruise this time.

I slam the back door, and she shrieks at me again. I know how this'll go if she calls the sheriff. He'll hold that one drunk and disorderly charge against me, will believe whatever she says, and then I'll end up in the clink. Won't be anyone here to take care of her.

Maybe she needs to see what'll happen if I'm gone. I don't want to go to jail though.

I stumble into the grass of my backyard, the air and light sprinkles cooling my skin. The woods at the back of our property are my refuge, one she never invades.

THE WHOLE STORY

Halfway across our weedy yard, my body slams into something, and I fly backwards onto my arse. What the hell was that?

I can't see anything and kick with my foot. It hits a solid wall, but nothing is there, well nothing I can see. I crawl to my feet and reach out. The surface is rough and uneven, like a bunch of large ropes wound together. I drag my hand around the outside of the object in a circle and take a deep breath of the earthy smell. Whatever it is about the size of a giant tree, and it starts at the ground and goes over six feet high.

Large drops pelt my face as I stare up towards the sky. It might even stretch up all the way into the thick dark rain clouds.

This is the spot where I vomited the other night after Denis gave me those pills that looked like beans. This is a beanstalk. An invisible beanstalk up to the giant world.

Sweet mother almighty. If I hadn't puked up those beans, would a beanstalk be growing out of my head right now?

No, of course not.

This is amazing. A beanstalk in my backyard. There's nothing else it could be. It's smaller than the ones the giants use, but those things are invisible too, except that somebody painted them. And there's a few others people have discovered, but who knows how many others are out there.

A beanstalk. Up to the giant land. And nobody will know about it. I can climb it to the top and check out the giant city. I'll have to do it at night 'cause otherwise people will see me floating in the air. Good thing we're on the edge of town.

I've never been up Kjempeland, never even gave them much thought since we see so few of them giants around here, but I've heard about a couple of them working on farms in the country. They're pretty strong since they're like double the size of us. And I've heard the stories about their gold.

They're probably stupid stories, but who knows. Maybe not.

As soon as night falls and Mumsy goes to bed, I'm going up to see if those rumors are true.

Chapter Four
Nissa

"Goodbye, Giselle." I give her a kiss goodnight, say goodbye to my parents, and head off to my job in Moorgan. In a few days, I won't be doing this anymore since I'll be at my own apartment living among the normies.

The stroll to the stalk is quick, as is the ride down. It's quiet now since it's after nine at night, but soon I'll be in the middle of chaos. I love the hustle and bustle of the ER and hope one day to go to school so I can be a nurse instead of a nurses' helper.

Mother and Father are supportive of my decision to live and work in the normie world. They see my struggles, and there's no possible way I can pursue my nursing dream up in Kjempeland anyway.

"Good evening, Nissa." Micki gives me a wave as I enter the ER. I couldn't have gotten a better nurse to work under. She's patient and explains so much to me that by the time I do attend nursing school, I'll most likely be ahead of the other students.

We do a little chit-chat, and then she sends me back to give one of the patients a bath. He's covered in blood, which fortunately is not his own. He apparently was butchering a pig and slipped and bumped his head. All is well, but he's a mighty mess.

"I need help. Where is everybody?" a man yells from the other room.

I peek my head out to see the front desk is empty. The receptionist runs around the corner and apologizes.

"What kind of hospital is this?" The man shakes his fist in the woman's face. His finger is bent at an unnatural angle, and bloody scratch marks mar his arm.

The receptionist talks quietly to him, but the man doesn't settle down. "I need to see the doctor. And call the sheriff. They're never around when you need them."

A nurse dashes out to help, and they escort the grumbling man into the room next to mine.

"Giants," he roars. "Cursed giants. They shouldn't be allowed down here."

The door shuts, and I can't hear much anymore, so I return to the stinky room to give the pig man a bath.

Giants and normies get along for the most part, but there are always bad apples out there, and some normies are afraid of giants because they think we're crazy beasts.

THE WHOLE STORY

Not many people here at work know I'm a giant, and I prefer to keep it that way. It's not that I'm ashamed of my heritage, but life is easier without people knowing.

When I have a free moment, I'll have to see what the man's problem was.

The night is hectic, so I don't have time to ask Micki about the guy who was complaining about giants. I saw the sheriff show up though and not long after, the sheriff escorted him out of the hospital.

After our shift is done, Micki and I walk together on my way to the lyft, since her home is in that direction too. The early morning air is crisp, and I love the quiet before people fill the streets on their way to work.

"Did you hear about that guy with the broken finger?" I ask. "The one complaining about a giant?"

Micki laughs. "The twit was drunk. Apparently, he ended up implicating himself. He started a fight with a giant at the tavern and broke two of his fingers when he hit the poor guy."

"So the giant did nothing?" The relief floods me. I can't let it bother me when a giant I don't know hurts somebody, but I feel responsible for some reason, and then I have to deal with the scared and angry normies.

"No. The sheriff took the guy to the drunk tank." She eyes me for a few seconds. "It was just another idiot who had to try prove how brave he was."

"There's too many in this world." We have our own like that up in Kjempeland too. I stifle a yawn. "I'll be glad when I don't have to make this commute anymore." Micki is one of the few who know I'm a giant, her and a couple of my bosses.

"Are you excited to move?" Micki asks.

"Yes."

But I'm scared to live on my own for the first time ever. Not to mention I won't see Giselle every day, won't hear her sing when she's taking a bath, or won't push her on her swing set after she's home from school. And I'll miss the small things like curling up on the couch and listening to Father tell us stories from when he was growing up or listening to Giselle jabber while I braid her hair.

"I felt the same way when Roger proposed. It's a huge step for you, but you're ready." Micki stops and takes my arm. "And honestly, Nissa. You're more mature than most girls your age. So many of those student nurses from the school are lazy. They have no idea what it takes to work in a hospital, and they know so little about the real world or what's outside their parents' houses. You're ready, and you'll do fine on your own."

THE WHOLE STORY

"Thanks."

My parents tell me the same thing, but there's always been the niggling thought in the back of my mind that they're saying those encouraging words because they're supposed to. Hearing it from a third party makes me feel better though.

We reach Micki's house, she gives me a wave, and I continue on to the lyft.

In one day, I'll be a full-fledged adult, be out on my own, be the only one responsible for my life.

And I'll be just fine.

Chapter Five
Basil

I sneak through my backyard in the dark of night. What am I doing? It's my backyard, so nobody will question me. The neighbor's houses are dark, and nobody can see me from the street anyway.

I get to the spot where I think the beanstalk is at and reach out my arms so I don't bang into it again. My hands touch the scratchy stalk. Who knows if it actually goes all the way up. I assume it does, but I can't see it. Hopefully the climb will be worth the work. Just to get a glimpse of all that gold.

I wouldn't steal it from someone like me, someone who has nothing, but if they really have rooms full of gold, they won't miss a few pieces.

One piece of giant gold could buy me so much. I could replace Mumsy's coin, and maybe replace some of my worn clothes, some of Mumsy's, or buy some decent food. I'm not sure how I'll explain it to her though. Maybe she won't notice.

THE WHOLE STORY

I trail my hand up as high as I can and gaze up into the sky. It could take forever to get to the clouds. I have no idea how long of a climb this could be. I look back at our tiny house. This trip is not just for me: it's for Mumsy too. Last year when she went to the doctor, I know there was other medicines that could help her better than the ones she takes, but they're too expensive. And the doctor had also mentioned someone who might be able to help Mumsy's body work better, a therapist he called it. Once Mumsy feels better, then I could get back to work. And working will get us better food and make Mumsy even healthier.

Yes. I have to do this for Mumsy, for us.

I throw my backpack over my shoulder and search for a foothold. It only takes a second to find a strand to step onto. I reach up and grasp the stalk with my hands and climb on the ridge. I slowly inch up the strand in a counter-clockwise direction as it winds around the stalk.

The strands are at least two feet in diameter and easy to hold on to. I consider looking down—I don't think I'm afraid of heights—but I've never been up higher than Denis' roof, so best not to test that theory now. I climb hunched over, grasping the strands so I don't fall. Don't look up, don't look down.

Sometimes I've watched the beanstalk cars run up to the top, but I have no idea how tall the beanstalks are.

All I know is that if I fall off the edge, I will end up in a pile of broken bones and blood on the ground.

My tense muscles need a break, my deep breaths taking a toll. The chill air helps cool me down, but I'm still sweating like a pig. I grab the strand and slowly twist around to lower to my arse, allowing myself to finally take a peek.

Sweet mother almighty. The town's lights sparkle below me like I'm above the stars this time. But the real stars are above me too, and I spot some of the constellations Melina taught me about. I'm swimming in a pool of twinkling lights, and I've never seen anything so spectacular. I can't help but sit and stare at the surrounding world.

The anxiety melts away, and I continue up, having lost all sense of time. It could be an hour or two I've been up here, but I'm not really sure.

Suddenly the light below me disappears, and I'm in darkness. The smell of earth envelopes me, and I continue going. I feel like I'm in a box with no way out, the air heavier.

My head smacks into something hard, and I reach up to run my hand over a solid surface. I pray there's a hole here 'cause if not, this work will be for naught.

I have to continue around the stalk, but on the other side, my hand slips through an opening, and I feel solid

THE WHOLE STORY

ground around the hole. I can't see anything though and push my hand farther through the space, hitting something scratchy. Branches. Some type of bush.

This is it. I'm in Kjempeland with the giants.

I rock back on my arse, unsure if I should go on. I could be discovered any moment, and I have no idea what the giants would do, if they'd hurt me, or if they'd call the sheriff and throw me in jail.

I have no excuses ready for why I'm here, and I should figure out something good to tell somebody if I'm discovered. I'm just curious and wanted to see what was at the top of the stalk. That's the only story I got. I don't know any giants here, have no reason to be up here.

I came all this way though, and I'm not going back down without looking around.

I pop my head up into the bush, avoiding the barbed branches, and pull myself out of the hole. I have to crawl through the bush on my hands and knees until I hit fresh air.

The sky above me opens up to a thousand shining lights, more than I've ever seen down below.

Not just thousands, millions. I see one of Melina's constellations, and then another. Why do they have so much more up here? Nobody knows how our worlds work, how the giants live above us but somehow the sun and stars shine through their solid ground, but it's amazing.

I take everything in for a while, the mystery and the wonder of it all, before I remember there's so much more to explore.

Lamps light up the street, similar to the ones I've seen in the wealthier neighborhoods below, and the monstrous houses tower around me. I've only seen a few giants, and never up close, but they're like twelve feet tall, so the towering houses make sense.

But they're not just large size-wise. They're similar to the mansions in Geld and Reichtum with their fancy porches and ornate doors, and there's lots of rooms behind all those windows.

The stories are probably true about the coin, probably overflowing with gold.

I wander through the backyards, hiding in the shadows, but there isn't much movement anywhere.

Not until a door slams. I slip behind a tree and watch. Two younger guys, close to my age from the looks of their faces, loaf on a front porch. It appears bright yellow under the light, and the house is green—a weird combination. The boys are well-dressed though, and even from my hideout, I can tell they are at least four feet taller than me. I should be nervous, but I'm not.

THE WHOLE STORY

"Tell him to move his arse," one guy hoots. "We don't have all night."

The second guy yells into the house, but I can't hear a response. "He's getting a bottle of scotch from his parents," the guy says.

"He's swiping it from his parents?"

My ears perk up. These boys remind me of myself in my earlier years.

"They'll never notice."

How can they not notice? All the lights are on in the house, and the kid is clunking around. Unless… his parents aren't home to catch him. Which means after they leave, I can go see what a giant house is like and maybe search around for that gold.

If Mumsy gets extra help, then she'll get better, and then I can maybe get out of the house and live my own life.

The last boy pops out the front door with the largest bottle of liquor I've ever seen, and they leave. I wait a few more minutes, watching the now dark house. The neighborhood is still, so I creep towards the house towering over me. The door is huge, the windows are huge, even the step is about double the size of the ones down below.

SUZI WIELAND

At the door, I scan the surrounding yards for people but see nothing, so I grab the doorknob and slowly twist—it's open.

I push the heavy door and quickly slip inside. Sweet mother, the ceiling is high. I feel like a mouse in this place, but hopefully I haven't walked into a trap.

No—the house is empty, it has to be from the way they talked. Even though it's dark out, the moon and stars outside provide enough light through the large windows, and I creep around, amazed at the height of the giant furniture. It's basically the same as ours, except bigger. Well, and this stuff is way better quality than mine, although that doesn't take much.

Eventually I'll tell Denis and the others about the stalk, but I want a bit of time to explore up here myself. Besides, they'll ruin it. Show up drunk and probably cause trouble up here. No, it's better not to tell anyone about this place, and since Mumsy doesn't venture in the backyard much, she'll never find the stalk.

This place has a different room for everything. A room with a couch and additional seating, a separate kitchen with tall counters and cupboards I could never reach, a dining room with a table about the size of a stage, and a parlor with shelves of books. Puts my two-room shack to shame.

THE WHOLE STORY

I open a door on the side of the kitchen. Holy schmoly—an indoor privy. I touch the smooth white porcelain and sigh. I've heard of them but have never seen one. No chamber pots, no freezing your arse in winter. I could live with this.

But that's not why I'm here. I need to find their room of gold and get home. I've checked the rooms down here, and the only thing remotely close to gold is a statue, so time to go upstairs. I stare up the steep steps to the landing above. I've climbed that lofty stalk, and now I have to trudge up these tall steps. My legs will be sore tomorrow.

At the top of the steps, I grab onto the railing and study my climb, huffing and puffing. No wonder not many normies come up to Kjempeland. Between the grand furniture and oversized things, I'm not sure how a normie could live like this.

Down the hall is another privy and four bedrooms. Four—what I wouldn't give for my own bedroom. Two of the rooms obviously belong to children, and the third must belong to the boy I saw.

I go back to the top of the stairs and stare down to the floor below. If I were a giant, where would I keep my gold? Either the bedroom or the parlor.

I run back to the bedroom that has to belong to the parents and try lug open the heavy drawers on the dresser. Maybe there's gold in there. First I'll get Mumsy an appointment with a good doctor, maybe even a therapist. Then I'll work on getting new clothes or better food. I could turn the gold into more coin down at the District, and me and Mumsy could find a better place to live. One with two bedrooms or maybe even an indoor privy.

My heart beats wildly as I tug at the drawer. It jerks open, and I stumble backwards. No gold. Just bloody boxes full of papers.

I check the other drawers, but find nothing and retreat downstairs. They have to be storing their gold somewhere.

The boys had talked of liquor. A drink would be refreshing right now. Just one or two though 'cause I don't want to be drunk when I climb down the stalk.

The chair scrapes along the floor as I drag it to the counter. I feel like a kid again, scaling the counter to get a special treat. The glasses are thick and heavy, and I can't fill it full, or I won't be able to hold it.

The pantry holds the liquor shelf, and I struggle to get the large bottle down. Finally I'm able to take a sip of the giant whiskey. It's okay, but nothing better than what I've had before.

Maybe I should try another.

THE WHOLE STORY

I take down two more bottles. The largest one is awkward in my hands, and I'm extra careful not to spill. The third bottle is the smoothest rum I've ever had, and I take another sip. Denis would love this stuff.

The bottle is only half full, and it'll take up most of the room in my bag, but if I don't find that gold, this will be a terrific substitute.

Well, not terrific. I'd prefer the gold, but this rum is liquid gold. I leave the bottles on the table and go back to the parlor to examine that statue.

After moving a chair, I'm finally able to reach it. The bloody statue is too light though—no way it's gold. I put it back on the shelf.

I check all the drawers and the closet but find nothing. Where have they hidden their stash? Maybe the giants are like my neighbor Adrian, who buries his coin in his yard 'cause he doesn't trust the banks. I have no time, and no shovel, to dig into the ground though.

The rum will have to be it for this time. I'll come up again though, scout things out. I got lucky tonight with these people being gone, but I won't be so lucky next time. I need to plan and watch before I make my next move.

I return to the kitchen and snatch the bottle of liquor and head back to the stalk.

Chapter Six
Nissa

Today is the big day: moving day.

Work passes so incredibly slow, but now it's six a.m., and I'm back home.

"Good morning, sweetheart," Father says as I rush into the kitchen.

I inhale the delicious coffee smell. His brew is stronger than the stuff the normies make, and I'll miss it.

And I'll miss him even more.

"Good morning, Father."

A cup of coffee waits at the table for me. He's always up when I get home from work, even though he doesn't have to get out of bed until seven. I'll miss our quiet times together, the conversations we share. When I have enough money to build my own home, I'll make sure it'll be tall enough to accommodate my parents and sister, so that one day I can make coffee in the mornings for him.

He pushes a cardboard box towards me before I sit.

THE WHOLE STORY

"What's this?" I ask.

"Open it to find out." He gives me a sly grin.

I do as directed. A coffee pot. The tarnished copper no longer shines bright, the wood handle is worn from years of use, and the faint smell of coffee is present.

I can't take my eyes off it, the metal cool under my fingertips. It's so beautiful, so loved.

"It belonged to Mahmah. It's been in a box all this time, and I figured we should put it to good use."

I bite down on my trembling lip. We never met Mahmah because she died when my father was a child. According to my mother, he only has a few reminders of his mother, reminders he keeps private. He rarely talks about her, but the few times he has, I could see how much he misses her.

"Thank you, Father. I'll take good care of it." I fling my arms around him and hug him tightly, and he pats me on the back.

After releasing him, I pick up the pot. It's fairly light in my hands. Giant coffeepots are one thing that is more similar to normie size since we make it so strong and usually drink less. It's slightly larger than a normie's, but not by much. I can't wait to get it into my apartment for my morning coffee. The stuff at the hospital is so weak that it tastes like water.

"I'm sure you will. Now sit down and enjoy your coffee before the little terror gets up." He winks, and I take the chair beside him.

My apartment is furnished, so I don't have a ton to move: mostly clothes, kitchen utensils, and other random things. Father and I just made our first trip down, and on the next, we'll bring Mother and Giselle, who is itching to see my place. The plan is to make our second trip after lunch, and then I'll get a few hours to sleep.

Giselle chatters the whole time Mother makes lunch, until she tells Giselle to run and get Father, who is outside talking to one of the neighbors.

He steps inside with a serious face, Giselle trailing him.

"Did you see anything unusual when you came home this morning?" Father asks me.

What does that mean? "No. It was a normal morning."

"I was talking to Knut. The Iversons were gone overnight, and when they returned home, it looked as if somebody had been rifling through their drawers. There were several bottles of liquor sitting out, and two were missing."

"It was probably Nils." That boy likes to party.

THE WHOLE STORY

"That's the thing," Father says. "Nils fessed up to taking a bottle of scotch, but they're missing a bottle of rum too. And he denies leaving the other bottles out."

Mother glances down at Giselle with her worried face. "They know for sure it wasn't the boys?"

"It has to be Nils and his friends," I say. "They're fools. They were probably drunk and don't even remember."

"That's possible." Father nods. "That boy gets away with everything. Knut was wondering though if you'd seen anything."

"No. Nothing."

"We should keep the door locked at night." Mother takes a long drink, her gaze set on Giselle.

"You're probably right. That means you too at your new apartment, Nissa." Father points his finger at me, and I roll my eyes. Kjempeland is pretty safe, but I know Moorgan isn't like home.

Giselle shoots up in her seat. "When are we leaving?"

"As soon as you're done with the dishes," Mother says, and Giselle deflates.

She's so darn slow, and it'll take forever. "I'll help you, squirt. Then we can get going sooner."

She brightens up and starts talking about Nils' little brother, a boy her age who is following in his troublemaker brother's footsteps.

It isn't long before we're on our way to my apartment with the second load. Down in Moorgan, we get a few curious looks. There's probably some people worried that the giants are moving into their town, but it doesn't happen that often. Sure, giants can build larger houses, but that doesn't help when they need to go out and about town.

Giselle steps into my apartment and glances around. "It's tiny."

Father chuckles, and I pat her on the shoulder. I suppose it is, but it's just me living here.

"But Father can't even fit," she harrumphs.

"I know. That's why I need to set these suitcases down so I can sit on the couch." He has to crouch down; otherwise his head will hit the ceiling. Mother is fine though since the ceilings are ten feet high, but she still has to watch out for the light fixtures and duck through the doorways.

"We'll give Nissa a week, and then maybe you can come back and visit her." Mother sets down her bags and joins Father, their bodies looming large on the miniature couch. I almost giggle at the sight.

"We have to leave now?" Giselle whines.

"No, we'll stay for a while, but then she needs to sleep before work."

Giselle wrinkles up her face and glares at me. "But I get to come back in a week?"

"Yes," I laugh at her scowl. "You can stay with me overnight if you want."

I get my family a few drinks, and we relax for a short time before they have to go.

Chapter Seven
Basil

"That rum is da bept." Denis leans against the tree trunk and squints at the sun peeking through the branches. We're lounging in the trees behind my house. I can't see the stalk, but I know it's there.

I thump down on the ground. The bark of the tree behind me scratches my arms, but I don't care. "What the hell you talking about?"

"The bept." He pops up and giggles. "Bept.... Wait—be-be-bessst." He slurs the word. "And you're the bept for sharing it with me." He raises his hand to give me a high slap, except only the edges of our hands hit 'cause we're so stinking drunk.

"Yeah, like I'd share it with those other a-poles." I take another swig of the rum. I've got a ton of buddies, but Denis is the one who's always there for me.

"We need to find that guy again to get more of this stuff."

THE WHOLE STORY

I told Denis some guy at the District gave it to me in payment, and I put it into a more manageable bottle. He can't know the truth. Not yet at least.

"Absolutely. I'll look for him again." Even though I'll never find him 'cause there is no him.

"Okay. One more drink, and then we're done. I'm pretty sure my boss wants them walls I build to be straight."

"One more then." He's got all evening to sober up, but this job of his is a good thing, and he doesn't want to mess it up. "Pass me that bottle, a-pole."

He laughs and hands it over.

I spend my next two days in Kjempeland, hiding in the bushes and scoping out the houses near my stalk. The house closest only has a kid and two parents, who all disappear early morning.

The house across the street, which is probably the largest of the four, has a gal about my age, a hot little number, well, for a giant, and she wears these tiny skirts that about show her arse, and those low-cut shirts. When I'm hiding under the bushes, I kinda forget how small I am compared to them.

House number three next to that has an old biddy with an unpredictable schedule. I don't want to be in her house 'cause she could show up at any time. House number four has an itty bitty baby and two adults. The mum is sometimes home during the day too, so that house might be out. My best options are the ones right by my hiding spot and across the street.

So on day three, I get up extra early and crawl up the stalk to hide under the bush and watch. The father leaves first, and then the mum and daughter go. I can't get over how brightly colored these houses are, and all the different colors. This block holds houses that are every color of the rainbow. In fact, from my view, I can't even see two houses that are the same. It was kind of weird at first, but I'm starting to like it now.

I wait a half hour, scanning the other houses for signs of life. The old biddy next door is gone, so now's a good time.

The lime green back door of the purple house is open, and I almost whoop for joy. Me and Mumsy never lock our doors 'cause we ain't got stuff worth stealing, but the rich folk in our town have plenty, and they probably lock their doors.

I slip inside and shut the door quiet, listening and watching, but there's no movement. First a survey of the house to get the general layout, making sure I duck under the low windows. It's daytime, and somebody passing by could see me.

THE WHOLE STORY

I kneel down and run my finger over the shiny smooth wood floor. It's nothing like the gouged up, scratched, and stained floor in our shack. No rotting planks that need to be changed periodically.

A mouth-watering sweetness fills the air, and in the kitchen I find a dozen giant-sized blueberry muffins on the counter. The muffin melts in my mouth, the blueberries sweet on my tongue, and I can barely finish half. The last time I had a muffin was years ago—they're not something I can splurge on right now. Sugar is expensive.

I have things to do and shouldn't be chowing down on giant muffins though.

As I roam through the house, I check any and every drawer but find nothing again. Maybe this whole gold story is a fake. The heavy closet door swings open in my hands, thick and solid like every door in the house. Inside, on a shelf, is a heavy metal box with a lock on it. Bingo!

No key is lying about, so I'll have to carry it home. There has to be something good in here. With a bit of coin, I could double it down at the District and then take care of Mumsy better.

My search of the parents' room comes up flat, and so does the other two bedrooms. One room left.

SUZI WIELAND

The daughter's room has all sorts of girl stuff on the walls and mirror. A plush comforter covers her large bed, and for half a second I consider crawling in and sinking down in those puffy pillows and blankets, snuggling in with the stuffed dog perched at the top of the bed. But with my luck, I'd fall asleep, and they'd find me here. A big no to that.

The first dresser drawer holds shirts, and on the second one, I suck in a hard breath at the silky brassieres and panties folded in dainty squares. The fabric is smooth, and I can't help but lift out a pink brassiere with black polka dots. None of the girls I know would have something so fancy.

That girl, whose room this is, has long brown hair and slender legs. And her chest. I can imagine stuffing my head into those pretties. My mouth waters like a rabid dog, and my dong stirs.

I've never thought of banging a giant. All that soft skin to touch, full round jugs, and the wonders they could do with their lips. I should ask around the District to see if anyone has, but I don't want to put suspicion on myself.

Bloody hell. I hope this woody goes away before I climb down the stalk. I stuff the pink brassiere in my bag. I didn't come here to take a woman's privates. I need to find that gold, and the only thing here is clothing.

THE WHOLE STORY

But wait—a small purple string sticks out between the shirts. I lift them up and find a velvet purple sack that jingles.

Could it be?

Sweet mother almighty—it's filled with gold coins. I dump them on my palm. One, two, three… eleven. Eleven gold coins. There's so much I could buy with this, so much I could get Mumsy.

The giant girl won't notice a few coins missing. I stuff some in my bag. These giants hide their gold well, and I've got to keep looking. I finger the remaining coins. If I took these too, I could get Mumsy better food, more meat, which would make her stronger. I shouldn't be taking this, but the giants are wealthy, and I'm sure they probably donate coins to those who need it. And nobody needs it more than Mumsy.

The other coins go in my bag. Hell, I should take the bag. That way she'll think she lost it. Mumsy will probably like it too. We never have extra coin to buy special things. I toss the velvet sack into my own bag and zip it up.

I'd better get going now.

Somebody is at the front door of the house across the street, and I duck back. They go inside, and I wait until I can safely sneak to my stalk.

The metal box makes for an awkward climb, and it goes slow, but I finally get down to safety. I hide the box back in the trees to be opened at a later time and bring my bag into the house.

Mumsy is snoring heavily on the couch, so I scramble up into my loft and dump out the contents. The gold pieces will stay in the purple bag, which I slip under my pillow. Mumsy can't make it up ladder, so no worries about her finding the gold.

The polka dot brassiere lays there, and I finger the soft fabric. Big jugs, little jugs—they're all good. I stuff the brassiere away 'cause it's making me randy. Maybe I should find a girl to call on. I have several go-to girls when I'm looking for fun. Geralyn maybe—no she's at work. Hedy's always up for fun, but she's with her boyfriend again, not like that matters to her, but I don't want to deal with him if he finds out.

Eva with her plump jugs and nice curves. She showed up again at Denis' looking for me one day. That's who I'll find. I've got time before I need to make lunch, so hopefully Mumsy won't wake before I get back.

Chapter Eight
Nissa

After a few days in my new apartment, I've made my list of things I forgot, and I want to go home to get them. I could probably slip back without anyone knowing since Mother and Father are at work, and Giselle's in school, but I need to sleep after a long shift at work. Besides, Mother won't mind if I just show up. Best not to make it a habit though, otherwise Giselle will expect me back all the time.

After getting some rest, I take the lyft up to Kjempeland and walk to my house. Everybody should be home now since it's about dinnertime.

I fling open the door and shout. "Guess who's home?"

Giselle lounges on the floor with a puzzle, and she jumps up and runs into my arms. "You're back." She about squeezes the life out of me, not realizing how strong she's getting.

"I forgot some stuff, so I thought I'd stop by and get it. Where's Mother and Father?" Usually at this time Father would be in the kitchen making dinner while Mother plays with Giselle.

She settles back down and searches through her puzzle pieces with a furrowed brow. "They're across the street. Something happened with Dina."

"Is she okay?" I peer out the window. Dina is on the front steps by herself, but I don't see my parents.

"I think so. Mother wouldn't let me go over there with them." She plucks out a puzzle piece and sticks it into the correct spot with a wide smile.

"I'm going over there to check on her, okay? I'll be back in a few minutes."

"Mmmm," Giselle murmurs, so I slip out.

Dina stares down at the leaf in her hands, ripping it into thin strips. She's in her first year of college, on her way to being an accountant. We used to be closer in school, but between my unusual hours at my job and her university classes, it's hard to find time together.

"Hey," I say tentatively. She looks okay, except for her dour expression. I spot my parents through the window sitting with hers in their living room.

"Nissa, hi." Her face brightens. "How's your new apartment?"

THE WHOLE STORY

I take a seat next to her on the steps, and she still towers over me. She's pretty tall for a female giant, about eleven feet.

"Good. It's quiet with no Giselle." Lonely, even though it's only been three days.

She laughs. "I can't wait to get out of the house too. Mum and Pop said I could live in university housing next semester. Mum didn't want me to, but Pop finally convinced her."

"You'll love it." Dina's an independent girl too, so I'm sure she'll fit right in. "So, what's going on?"

Dina's face darkened. "Did you hear about what happened at Nils' house a few days ago?" She pauses a moment to wait for me to respond and continues. "I came home this afternoon and found a half-eaten muffin in the kitchen. I thought maybe Mother had to leave in a rush, although that's not like her, and I went up to my room, and my dresser drawers were not quite closed. I have this velvet bag with my savings hidden in there, and it was gone. All my gold coins."

"Somebody was inside your house?" Just like Nils. I glance over at our house across the street with my little sister inside. This is suddenly becoming more real. "And they stole your gold?"

How dare they break in and take her things. I'm about to ask if her parents had anything stolen, but she lets out a shudder.

"That's not the worst of it. He dug through my undie drawer and stole one of my brassieres. My favorite pink one with black polka dots. I want to throw away the whole drawer. Who knows what he touched."

"You're kidding?"

Her lip curls. "It's gross."

My own skin crawls. I wouldn't want someone sneaking through our home like that, someone touching my things. "When did it happen?"

"Sometime when I was at my classes."

"That's strange. Must be someone different from Nils' though. They broke into his house at night." But how weird that two things happened in the same week around here.

"I know, but it's an odd coincidence." She sprawls back on the step and stares up at the blue sky. "It's going to suck because now my parents will be weirded out about everything. They'll probably find an escort to bring me home after school and check out the house."

"Do you know how much coins they took?"

"Not exactly. I had maybe twelve pieces. I don't know. And I was saving up for something special too." She sighs. "The constable took the report, but there's not much they can do since nobody saw him. They're going to keep a watch out in the neighborhood for a while though."

"That's good." Our neighborhood is generally pretty safe, and I want it to stay that way.

Chapter Nine
Basil

Denis folds his hands behind his head and leans back in his chair, patting his stomach. He has to be as full as me after those juicy steaks we had. I've never eaten meat so tender I could cut it with a fork.

"Can you imagine the people who eat like this all the time?" I ask. I bet giants always eat steak with tangy sauces and liver pate with crackers and drink that fancy rum we finished off last week. Their fruit is probably always fresh, their bread never moldy.

"No kidding. I could get used to this." Denis stretches out his arm and fingers the fabric on the new white shirt I bought him. We couldn't go to a restaurant like this in our regular rags, so we stopped at a store for new clothing. "What's the plan after dinner? We can't waste our new look drinking in the woods. I think we can get into the lounge up the street with these threads."

THE WHOLE STORY

No way would they let us in the way we usually dress. I pat my pocket and feel the normie coin I got when I traded those gold pieces.

"We need some company though."

He raises his brow in question.

We've got three choices.

We can go find Eva and another girl. But that means we'd have to spend more coin on dressing them up too, and that'll bring on a whole lot of questions I don't want to answer.

We can try pick up girls who belong in this part of town, but they might expect us to lay out too much coin. Those girls also tend to be bossy, plus, they might realize where we live, and they won't like that. Then at the end of the night, who knows if they'll put out.

We can hire uptown girls. They'll dress all fancy like they belong here too, but they can't complain if we buy them the cheap drinks. We'll have to pay for sex, but it'll be worth every coin.

"Let's go to the BoomBoom," I say.

"You sure?" Denis tries to hide the excitement on his face.

"Yeah. This is our special night out." I motion to the waiter for another drink. We deserve some fun with the way our lives suck. And besides, Denis has been working fourteen-hour days.

A half hour later, we stand at the front desk of the BoomBoom, negotiating our prices with the madam for the girls we picked. She goes into another room for something, and Denis turns to me with a smirk. "I'm starting to see a pattern."

"What are you talking about?"

He flicks his head towards the girl I chose. "Long brown hair, dark skin. Braids. Like the last two girls you flirted with."

Sweet mother almighty. He's right. This girl. The others I'd been hitting on and dancing with at the bar, they all look similar to Nissa. I kinda forgot about her, but obviously I haven't.

"Huh. Didn't even notice." Boy, if I run into her again, I'll have the coin to take her out somewhere nice. Maybe not the place Denis and I ate at, but something decent.

The madam shoots around the corner and waves the girls over. Britt is my girl. She wraps her long arms around my waist and presses her jugs into my chest. She smells sweet. "So what are we doing tonight, gentlemen?"

Crikeys. She does look like Nissa. Not her face, but from behind, it'd be easy to mistake the two. My head goes fuzzy as her fingers tickle my lower back.

THE WHOLE STORY

"Uh, maybe we should get a room here before we go out," I blurt. That wasn't in the original plan, but my dong is coming alive.

The madam clutches my arm with her boney hand. "Okay, that'll be additional coin. Paid up-front."

I don't want to pay more, especially after everything we laid out for these two, but Denis is looking at me expectantly, and Britt's fingers have untucked my shirt from my trousers and are touching my skin. I can't take back my suggestion now, and I don't want to.

I dig in my pocket and give the woman the coin.

"Room two-twelve. You have an hour." The madam disappears.

Britt smiles at me big. "Let's go have some fun, boys."

I wake up the next morning in my loft, a hammer thumping my head. Or at least that's how it feels. I spent way too much coin on those girls last night. They had expensive taste in drinks, and then we ordered food at the lounge.

But holy schmoly. Britt did anything and everything I wanted. And Denis' girl too—what was her name anyway? I can't remember now. Can't remember how many times we banged them over those six hours.

I reach under my pillow for the purple velvet bag and shake out the remaining gold. Two coins! I shoot up and bang my head on the ceiling. Bloody hell. I move to where the ceiling is higher and rub the sore spot.

Only two gold coins are left, and I'm not sure where the others went. They disappeared way too fast. Mumsy has been eating better, and I paid back the coin I gambled away, but I can't believe it's almost gone now. I'd only wanted to spend a little on something special, to treat Denis and myself, and now it's almost gone. How stupid I am.

Today is laundry day, and I have washing to do, but after that, I'm heading down to the District to make back a bit of the coin I've spent. Then I'll go buy Mumsy a new sweater so she doesn't always have to wrap herself up in a blanket when the house gets drafty.

I grab the polka dot brassiere and breathe the scent in—it still smells like the giant girl's room. I have to show this to Denis, tell him I found it on the street. He'll get a kick out of it.

I can sneak it out in the wash and then bring it to my hiding spot in the woods. No way I'll show him here in the house. Mumsy will yell at him if he comes inside.

The brassiere is so smooth and soft, just like the brassieres the BoomBoom girls wore. Do giants have uptown girls too? I'd probably have to pay out of the nose for that, but it'd be worth it. My trousers tent up at the image of a giant Britt and her friend, and I wank off once again.

Laundry can wait a few more minutes.

Chapter Ten
Nissa

I straighten my dress as I stare into the mirror. Over the last six months I've been working at the hospital, I've been asked out by several different men, but dating a normie was too much of a hassle since I lived in Kjempeland. But I don't live there anymore.

Dietrich is meeting me at the Canteen in fifteen minutes, so I finish getting ready and leave. The walk only takes me five minutes, and when I arrive, I find him already there too.

Prompt. I like that.

"Nissa, hello." He gives me this sweet smile and pulls the chair out for me. He's got such pretty brown eyes and curly brown hair—I'll admit I'm a sucker for curls.

Within minutes, we're making small talk about my nurses' aide's job and his veterinary position at the large cattle farm outside of town.

THE WHOLE STORY

"We're the largest operation in the region," he says proudly. "I bet this restaurant serves our steak."

"Are you the only vet there?"

"No," he chuckles. "It's a huge facility with other animals too. I'm actually one of the assistants to the head vet, but there are several men who work under me."

"I never gave much thought to where our meat comes from. I'm sure it's quite a process." I've been to several family farms in Kjempeland, but the way we raise our farm stock at smaller facilities is so different from the normie's large farm stations.

"It's boring actually. I mean, the raising them part is. I bet you have interesting stories from the emergency department."

"There's always something crazy going on. I love how every day is different." There are always new and interesting cases to learn about, and I rarely have boring downtime to pass by.

Lunch passes so quickly, and soon he offers to get dessert out on the Riverwalk, one of my favorite outdoor spots in Moorgan. A lazy breeze blows as we amble down the wooden sidewalk adjacent to the busy river. We have no river in Kjempeland, and I can't get enough of watching the different boats riding the river, from barges to small rowboats.

People crowd the shops and outdoor food booths, and a riverboat with an enormous paddlewheel toots its horn. Giselle would love riding on a boat, or visiting the Riverwalk, and she'd probably want to stop at every food booth out here, just to try everything.

"Dietrich," a man calls, and an older gentleman approaches us. The smile grows on Dietrich's face, and the two men shake hands before he turns to me.

"Nissa, this is a friend of mine, Frantz. He works for the Cattlemen's Association, an organization I belong to."

Frantz offers his hand. "Nice to meet you, Miss Nissa." Then he turns back to Dietrich. "Have you started your letter-writing campaign? It's imperative that the councilmen see why the Trade Act will harm our city."

"Yes, I've already sent off my letter, as have others at our facility. I've been speaking with some of the smaller cattle farms around too."

"Good, good." Frantz pats Dietrich on the back. "We thank you for your hard work. The vote is three weeks off, so we don't have much time." He tips his hat to me. "Good day, ma'am."

I can feel my face turn red. I'm not used to being called ma'am.

THE WHOLE STORY

"What's the Cattlemen's Association do?" I ask as we stroll down the walk again.

"We promote our industry and help the smaller facilities keep up on the latest standards."

"What's the bill he was talking about?" I don't keep up on politics in Kjempeland, much less in Moorgan. Maybe that's part of becoming an adult though.

Dietrich's face sours. "The giants. They're trying to break into our market and sell their inferior product."

He's got to be kidding. "There's nothing wrong with the giants' cows."

"Yes, there is. They raise their stock in deplorable conditions."

I clench my hands and try to temper my voice. I may not have visited a ton of farms, but I know many families who own them, and they're good people who care for their stock.

"That is not true. Have you ever been up to a farm in Kjempeland?"

"I've read multiple reports, and I've seen some of their product. Their meat is inferior, and they add harmful chemicals to preserve the meat. We don't know the effects of that—"

"No, we don't."

"We?" He takes a step back and eyes my whole body as if he thinks I'm a giant in disguise. And I guess I am.

"Yes, we. Giants believe in natural farming. They only use natural remedies for sick animals and—"

"See, you admit it. Their animals aren't healthy." He folds his arms and glares at me. "And since when do you side with the giants?"

"Side with the giants?" I stutter. We just met. He's making accusations about something he has no idea about, and he probably hasn't even taken the time to learn the truth, just listens to what other people tell him and regurgitates it. Anger bubbles up inside. "I am a giant, for your information."

"No, you're not." Dietrich crows.

"My parents are both giants. I happened to be born with different genes, so I'm normie sized."

The laugh falls from his face. "You can't be serious. Why would you lie to me?"

"I never lied to you. You never asked."

It shouldn't matter if I'm a giant. We've just met; we're going out on a date. One date.

"You're a doggone giant. That's not exactly something you hide from someone." He sneers at me. "No wonder you're defending their inferior products."

"I'm defending them because they're as good if not better than yours. Besides, it was only our first date." I stomp away, calling over my shoulder. "And now it's our last."

THE WHOLE STORY

Giants are like normies, only larger. Otherwise there's no difference between us. Why can't some people get that?

I try to control my shaking until I get away from him and sink down onto a bench. I've fallen into an easy complacency at my job, haven't told many people who I am, and I forgot how ignorant people could be. I don't want to live a life where I have to quiz people on how they feel about giants before I become friends with them.

Maybe I should have told him. Yes, it was only our first date, but marrying a normie would bring about a few difficulties when it comes to children. I don't want to think about that now, about how challenging life would be with a giant child in a normie world. But I deserve a chance at life, at love, and finding it up in Kjempeland is not a possibility.

It's too much to consider now, and I just want to get out and meet people and have fun.

I'd give anything to be a normal giant, to live up in Kjempeland with my friends and family, but I don't have much of a choice. My own world doesn't fit me, and so I'm down here, trying to live my life. I won't let Dietrich's ignorance get me down though. Most people are good, most people are accepting. At least that's what I hope.

Chapter Eleven
Basil

I can't believe the gold is gone. All of it. Every single piece.

"Another go-around?" Einar says, staring at the dice in my hand as I kneel on the side of the gravel road in the District. "Double or nothing." He offers a smarmy grin, and the oppressive heat in the alley smothers me, the buildings looming up around us blocking the breeze.

The other guys are yelling to go for it, but I shut out their voices and squeeze the dice burning a hole in my hand. I can do it this time. Make back all the coin I lost. But if I lose, I'll owe him even more. He already loaned me some coin, and I hate being in debt with him.

"Naw. I'm done for now." I toss him the dice, and the group groans.

"You've got a week." His face is serious, and I know I'll be in trouble if I don't pay it back. I really need to stick to my rule: no gambling more than what's in my pocket.

THE WHOLE STORY

"I will." I get off my knees and trudge away from the dirty streets of the District. Denis will be mad I lost the coin too. No more nights at the BoomBoom like I promised him.

Time for another trip up-top. I plan it out as I head towards home, out of the District and through the downtown. There's a bustle in front of the hospital, and I wait for people to clear the sidewalk. Too many wagons in the street with drivers who don't pay attention, so I'm not going to walk there.

Across the street is a park with two women sitting on a bench. The one woman's brown braids are pulled back behind her neck—she almost looks like Nissa, but doubtful it's her. I should go over and check though.

But why? I'm a foolish dunderhead who can't hold onto my coin. I'd had so much gold in my hands, and it's gone. She'd never want a guy like me.

I take one last glance at the Nissa-lookalike and head down the sidewalk. I don't deserve a girl like her anyway. Every step closer to home drives in that fact. From the houses to the people.

A kid, maybe ten, glances up at me from the yard down from mine. He's not wearing shoes, and his clothes are ragged, his face dirty. He sticks his tongue out at me before returning his attention to the toad in his grimy hands. He should be in school, but he's not 'cause his father is a drunkard and can't hold a job. Every shack on my street has a story, each one as bad as the other.

As soon as I get home, I make lunch for Mumsy, make sure she has her medicine, and find my bag to go up-top. If this next house is a bust, then I'll have to branch out farther from the stalk, which will make my trips more dangerous.

The climb up the stalk takes less time now that I'm getting used to it. The sky is cloudy, like it is down below, with thick gray billowing clouds. That stalk would turn into a slippery slide in the rain, so I'll have to get back if I see any drops.

I crouch in the scratchy bushes and scan the neighborhood. The house I'm stalking has a kid in school and two parents who work during the day. Should be an easy run. I'm not gonna be stupid this time and waste the gold. Mumsy comes first, and then me second.

The neighborhood is clear, so I sneak up to the house and go inside the unlocked door. I almost stumble over the shoes on the rug. Three sets. Wow—those men's shoes could crush my head in one stomp, although from the stories I've heard, giants aren't any more dangerous than we are.

The living area and kitchen are a bust, and I head for the closet in the parlor. The door creaks open, and I freeze, my muscles tight. The house is still though, so I need to relax.

Jackpot.

A tin can of gold and silver coins rests on the floor. On top is a thin plastic case displaying three coins. I slide the case into my back pocket and reach down and grab a bunch of loose coins. The cold heavy metal weighs down my hand, and I can't help grinning. This could last me for years, especially if I do it right.

And I will this time. I won't make those same mistakes. I'm going to get Mumsy a doctor and a therapist, one she's comfortable with. I'm not gonna gamble it away after I pay back Einar. No unnecessary purchases.

The can barely budges when I try slide it over, so I can't take the whole thing, but I can stuff as many coins in my bag and pants as I can carry. Maybe I can stand at the top of the stalk and drop down the coins, but they might dent the ground, and someone might notice the stalk. No, not a good idea.

I fill my pockets with coins and then my bag. Maybe me and Mumsy can get an apartment in the city, get away from the dirty ramshackle homes where we are now.

My own bedroom. And maybe a bathtub for Mumsy where she could wash herself. I can barely imagine it.

I grunt as I lift the bag, but I barely get it an inch off the ground, so I drag it across the floor. The thick canvas shouldn't rip as I lug it across the grass, and it'll take some maneuvering, but once I get onto the stalk, it'll slide easier.

I'll have to split the stash back at home. Keep a bit in the woods, and in different places around the house where Mumsy can't find it. She'd ask too many questions.

I swing the door wide open and peek outside. All's clear, so I grip the bag to heave it over the threshold.

"What the bugger?" a gruff voice booms.

Oh no.

A giant with fire shooting out of his eyes and wild red hair glares down at me from up the steps, the blue veins practically bulging in his face. My heart batters my chest.

"What are you doing?" He shakes an angry fist at me, a fist that's bigger than my head. He's going to stomp me like a bug, and Mumsy will be all alone. I'll never see Denis again. Oh crikeys, what was I thinking?

The bag slips out of my clammy hands, and I bolt towards the stalk, the coins in my pocket banging into my thigh. I pump my legs as fast as I can, the thunderous steps echoing behind me propelling me forward.

Go, go, go!

"Stop," he yells.

THE WHOLE STORY

I scramble through the bushes and into the hole, the giant sprinting behind me as he hollers, his deep voice vibrating in my chest. I crawl through the doorway and start down as fast as I can go. I don't want to fall, but I don't want to get caught. Which fate would be worse? Probably the giant.

I chance a look up. The giant is attempting to climb onto the stalk, but he's slow. I kick my speed up a notch, not knowing what I'll do when I get down. I need to hide.

After forever, my feet hit the ground, and I take off. At the shed, I stop. If I chop the stalk down, then he won't be able to find me. I can't see him, and I bet he went back up, too scared to climb down.

I have to chop the stalk.

The axe weighs down my hands, but I swing it with all my might even though I can't see the stalk. The blade carves out a chunk that hits my leg before flying to the ground, and I do it again.

And again.

And again.

Slowly the crevice widens. My arms are burning, but I can't stop. I'm close. So close. The stalk will fall away from the house and into the backyard and woods. My grip is tight despite my sweaty hands, and I continue swinging. I have to keep that giant from getting to Mumsy.

The stalk groans, and I swing again and miss. It's moving, leaning to the side now, and I jump back. It drops so slowly and smashes into the ground. A giant boom fills the air as dirt and branches blast my body. I shield my eyes and drop to the ground, my face slamming into the scratchy grass. I cover my mouth with my shirt to avoid breathing in all the dust.

A thundering crack echoes around the countryside, and I jerk my head up and gasp. A massive hole opens up in the sky, the ground up-top cracking apart towards the blue house. Dirt and trees fall through the air, and suddenly the house teeters on the edge of the hole.

Sweet mother almighty. I scramble to my feet and take off for the woods. Just as I cross into the trees, the world behind me explodes. I dive to the ground and hide behind the trees, coughing from the dust filling my nose. The earth continues to rumble around me until slowly the violent noises fall silent.

My eyes are so itchy, and after trying to rub them, I realize the axe is still in my hands, the gold coins in my pockets. I have to get rid of them. I stumble farther into the woods and use the blade to dig out a hole to bury them. My whole body is wet by the time it's done, my fingers covered in dirt, but the axe and the gold pieces from my pocket are hidden.

Oh no, Mumsy!

THE WHOLE STORY

I shoot out of the trees and around the fallen stalk into the dusty air. The brown stalk is now visible and stretches all the way to the house.

The house! Rubble smothers my smashed home, wood and glass and furniture and so many unrecognizable objects. Only one part of the roof sticks up in the air—but wait. That's where Mumsy's room once stood. Maybe she's okay.

I round a crushed giant couch and other debris to the corner of the house. "I'm coming, Mumsy. Hold on."

She has to be okay. If she was in bed. If nothing landed on her. If, if, if… There's too many ifs. I dig in the rubble, my hands raw and bloody. My chest is heavy, and my arms tired, but I can't give up.

Other people come to assist me, but I don't even look who. We dig and toss debris away. The noise increases around me, and large hands drag me backwards.

"No, Mumsy's in there. I have to help her." I try pull away, but they don't let me go.

"It's okay, son. Let us handle it. Do you know if she was in the house?" The man from the sheriff's department stares down at me with questioning eyes, and I finally take in the scene all around. People are working on the house, others milling around, a mix of sheriff's people and looky-loos.

"She's always in the house. I... I..." The other parts of the house are smashed to bits. "She's usually in her room." When she's not on our couch. I swallow the lump in my throat. That room is under the stalk, nobody could survive under the weight.

The man waves over a woman and practically throws me into her arms with instructions to help me. The blood runs down a deep cut in my arm, and for the first time I feel pain in my foot. My shoe is missing, and my toes are bloody.

"Come with me, young man," the woman says. "We'll help you out."

I don't know what to do, what to say. All I have is hope that Mumsy is okay.

Chapter Twelve
Nissa

"What was that noise?" I peek my head out of the patient room. We both heard it, an ungodly crack and boom. Some kind of explosion.

"I don't know," a passing nurse mutters, "but I'm guessing we'll be finding out soon."

I return to the young patient, who just needs someone to sit with until his mum or pop arrives.

"My cast is nifty," he says, admiring the white casing on his arm. "I can't wait to show my friends."

He reminds me of Giselle and how she was so proud when she broke her arm, but his pain meds will wear off, and then he won't be so happy.

"Yes, it is."

His mum rushes into the room and goes straight to her son and asks him a hundred questions, then she turns to me. I excuse myself to find a nurse since I'm not qualified to answer.

"Nissa," Micki calls as she zooms by me. "Come with me. Something's happened, and it'll probably get busy here."

"What happened?" I ask.

"I'm not sure yet," she calls, rushing down the hall.

The anticipation builds in the air, nobody knowing quite what's going on, but they even call in extra help. People rush around, surgery rooms are on standby. It's something significant.

Micki returns to stand by me, and a harried man dashes over. "A giant stalk on the east side of town has tipped over and ripped a hole in the sky."

What? I grip the edge of the desk and focus on his words. A stalk would crush anything it landed on, and the people inside the lyft. Hundreds could be hurt. My stomach rolls, sending a sour taste into my mouth. There will be death from this tragedy, but hopefully it's not a huge loss of life. But how can it not be? Those lyfts are in busy places with tons of people.

"It's a mess, but at least it happened in a quiet neighborhood," the man gulps. He steadies himself on the counter with his trembling hands.

"Wait," someone says. "Where did it happen? You said the east side? There is no stalk there."

"In the Willows. It wasn't one of the lyfts. It was an invisible stalk. Nobody seems to have known about it."

THE WHOLE STORY

Oh, thank goodness it wasn't a lyft filled with people, but there still could be many injured.

"Where's that neighborhood?" I ask Micki.

"It's kind of a poor area on the edge of town, right next to the woods," she whispers. "How could a stalk fall over? I didn't think…" Her voice quiets.

The stalks are so mighty, so sturdy, and I never imagined one could topple over. Never considered it on any of the hundreds of trips I made up and down.

"How many are hurt?" another person asks.

"I don't know for sure. The stalk seems to have fallen into the woods on the edge of town. They're trying to get to survivors. We'll find out soon."

A gloomy pall overtakes the room, and we wait to hear more news. Within minutes, a flurry of noise breaks through the front door, and they wheel in a patient on a stretcher. I can't see over the throng of people, but they take the stretcher back to the other room. Then a second one rushes in.

"Nissa, come with me." Micki waves me over, and we hustle to the first room. A team of doctors and nurses surrounds the woman, the dirt covering the red cuts across her skin. Micki sends me out for more towels, and I rush off.

Doctors and nurses crowd the second patient coming in, and I can't tell if it's a woman or man. I grab the towels and return, freezing at the sight in front of me.

Dirtied people fill the ER, sad faces, scared faces, but at least they're alive. Cries and chaos sweep through the room as hospital employees try to keep things under control. A woman coughs into her hands in the waiting area, her face black. Some of these people have probably lost loved ones, and my heart aches for them.

Two stretchers, bodies draped with a cloth push through the door. They're large, too large, their bodies hanging off the ends of the stretchers. I swallow the lump in my throat. Those are giants underneath those cloths. Someone from Kjempeland has lost loved ones, but I can't dare question if I might know them or if I know their families. Kjempeland has over five thousand people, and I can't let my worries slow me down. There's two fighting to survive right now, one who is waiting for these towels I'm carrying. I run off for the patient.

Micki smiles grimly when I return. "She's okay. This woman. She's alive." The atmosphere in the room is more relaxed but still busy, and I take a deep breath. The old woman on the bed doesn't look okay though, her frail body and sunken eyes underneath the dirt and cuts and scratches. Now that she's stabilized, a nurse works on cleaning her body.

THE WHOLE STORY

"She's unconscious, and she has a broken leg," Micki says. "But her heart-rate is fine, and she's breathing. Let's go see if we can help the others out."

I follow her into the other room and gasp. The doctor leans over the patient, pumping on her stomach. A nurse is holding the woman's limp wrist. Two dead giants, so far, and this woman may be next.

"Again," someone calls, and the doctor breathes into the woman's mouth. Her black hair is clumped together on her head, the blood marring her dark skin. Micki rushes up to help the other nurses, and I stand back. Another doctor gives commands, but her voice doesn't hold the hope it usually does when they know they can save a patient, and a nurse is whispering in the poor woman's ear, caressing her forehead.

They work on the woman until the doctor finally gives up. She shuffles to the side and blocks my view, but I'm pretty sure she made the sign of the cross on her chest.

The nurse at the top of the bed squeezes the woman's hand and wipes her tears away with her other hand. "She's just a child." She sniffs.

But she's larger than me. My heart breaks along with the others. This is a giant, a girl who'll never become an adult, never know the wonders of the world.

SUZI WIELAND

A somber pall fills the room, as we stand there with nothing to say, and finally the doctor steps away from the bed, her eyes filled with an anguish I've never seen.

I'm drawn towards the body of the poor girl who lost her life. Her family will be devastated. Or it could be her family under the draped clothes I saw earlier.

"This was in her arms when they brought her in," a nurse says from the back of the room. She trudges forward with a dour face, a brown bear with a red bow in her hands.

Giselle has a bear like that. Some family lost their child, a little girl like my sweet sister.

The nurse places the bear in the girl's arms and blinks her wet eyes. I step closer.

The brown curly hair is just like Giselle's, and those blood-soaked pajamas. They have rainbows on them… like Giselle's.

I can't breathe. It's a coincidence. It has to be.

I run to the bed. The nose is familiar, the chin—it belongs to me too. The bear and the pajamas and… I reach out and touch the puzzle piece pendant hanging on her neck, my hand trembling. Her body is still, and her lids closed, but I know the eyes underneath them.

"Nissa, what's wrong?"

Micki's words sound so far away, as if I've fallen into a deep hole, and I can hardly hear her.

THE WHOLE STORY

My squirt is gone.

My whole body shakes, my knees week, and tears flood my eyes. Screams fill the small room, and I know it's me, but I don't care.

My baby sister is dead on the table.

Micki has a tight grip on me on the couch, and I'm not sure I ever want her to let go. I don't want to emerge from this cocoon to face the world. Not only did I lose my sister but also my mum and pop. I watched their cloaked bodies be pushed through the ER, and I didn't even know it was them. I didn't know my own parents were dead. At some point I'll have to get up out of this couch and face the future of a life without the three people I love the most.

My throat is so thick; I don't even feel as if I can breathe. I'm not even sure I want to keep breathing with them gone.

"I'm so sorry, honey." Micki stokes my skin like Mother used to do when I was hurt. The sobs bubble up through my chest and burst out again. The man who taught me to never give up, the woman who took care of her friends as if they were her family, my little sister who couldn't stop talking… I'll never hear her voice again. Any of their voices.

SUZI WIELAND

And nobody can explain how my family is dead, why they're in this normie hospital, how they ended up here.

Nobody can explain how a beanstalk collapsed and how my family fell to their deaths.

Micki holds me as she has since I looked down upon the mangled corpses of my dead parents.

"Can I get you anything?" someone asks. I blink my wet eyes at her but can't recognize the face through my tears, and Micki gives her a quiet no.

My life is over. My family is gone, and I don't know what to do, who to talk to, what to say. My aunts and uncles and cousins need to be contacted, but I'm not sure how to say the words that'll destroy their lives like mine has been.

"Can I take you home now?" Micki asks.

"Home?" Oh god. I have no more home. It's gone, fallen through the air with my parents and sister. I gasp for breath, my whole body scorching. The room seems to have no air. I can't breathe.

Micki pulls me tighter and apologizes again, as if it's her fault my parents and sister are dead.

"How can she be gone?" I choke out. "I'm taking her to her HoneyBee campout this weekend. We're going to the woods and will roast marshmallows and sleep in the tent. And my parents, they were going away for the

THE WHOLE STORY

weekend. They haven't gone on a trip by themselves for so long, and now they can't go."

I close my eyes and lean my head back on the couch.

"Miss Lund," a man says from the doorway. He strides in and takes a seat. "I'm Deputy Dag Olsen with the sheriff's department. Are you able to talk?"

I sniff and wipe my eyes again, nodding. I don't want to think anymore about what I'm missing this weekend, what I'll miss for the rest of my life.

"I'm sorry for your loss." The compassion fills his face, but I can't feel it in my numb heart. "I've talked to a few witnesses, but I'll be talking to more. As best as we can presume, there was a stalk that nobody knew about. Somehow it tipped over and ripped a hole in Kjempeland right at the location of your family home. That's all we know right now."

"But how? How can there be a stalk nobody knows of? And how does a stalk tip over?"

"I don't know, but I can assure you we'll do everything we can to figure it out." The deputy stands. "I need to speak with other witnesses, but I'll be back." He gives me a sad smile and leaves the room.

Other witnesses. Maybe they'll have the answers I need.

It doesn't make sense, my family being home during the middle of the day. Giselle was wearing pajamas, so does that mean she was sick? That doesn't explain why both my parents were there though.

Karline, another nurses' aid, busts into the room and stares and me and Micki. "What's going on? Someone said you weren't feeling well."

"No, she's not feeling well," Micki says. She's about the only one who knows I've lost my family, my parents, and my squirt, and I don't want anybody else to know right now.

Karline studies my red eyes and wet face with suspicion. "Somebody thought you knew one of the victims or something."

My eyes pop open, and the bile rises up my throat. I don't want anybody to know who I am. It's stupid, but I don't want that right now. I can't deal with the questions, with the discomfort when they treat me differently.

Micki sighs. "If you must know, Miss Meddler, Nissa knows the old woman who survived. Now please shut that door on your way out and get back to work."

Karline frowns but slinks out the door.

"I'm sorry for lying," Micki says into the quiet room. "I didn't know what to say."

"It's okay." I hang my head. I'd rather hear those rumors fly than the others. My family was the only ones to die, but the old woman is in a precarious situation. My

THE WHOLE STORY

family's house landed on top of hers, and she's been injured badly. Luckily, nobody was hurt so badly, the ones with houses in the woods. "How is the woman?"

"She's still unconscious."

"Do you know anything about her?"

"Not a whole lot. Her name is Stella Hagen, and she's forty-five. Her house was in a neighborhood called the Willows—you didn't know where that is, right?" she asks, and I shake my head. "It's a poor area, the houses mostly shacks. I've driven through there before, and it's sad. Kids without shoes, some houses with electricity but no running water. That's about all I know. Her body is frail, but we're hoping she's strong inside. Those people are often fighters. They have to be to survive."

I want to hold onto that tiny bit of hope inside me that she'll be okay, but it's warring with the sorrow over losing my family.

"Can I see her?" Maybe her recovery will give me a little joy, that one life is surviving this tragedy.

"Yes, we brought her to second floor, room twelve. I'll take you there."

Micki brings me upstairs to one of the rooms that is filled with beds. With eight patients in this room, it should be noisier, and there always is a constant buzz in the air, but it's a quiet buzz of nurses whispering and running across the floor. The smells are overpowering though, body odor, antiseptic, and often vomit.

Many hours of my time are spent in these rooms cleaning and sometimes feeding people, and I always feel sorry for them. They're the ones who cannot afford their own room, so they're stuck here with everyone else.

"She's in the last bed on the right. Do you want me to stay with you?" Micki asks.

I know she will if I say yes, but it's time to let her go. In a few short hours I went from having a family to just me, and I need to learn how to stand on my own. The thought scares me, but I'm alone now, and I have no choice.

"Go ahead. I'll find you soon," I say, and give Giselle's bear a squeeze for strength.

She gives me a hug and rubs my back tenderly. Micki would be a terrific big sister. I hope Giselle thought I was a good big sister too.

Was she scared when she was falling to the ground? Did she know what was happening? The pain tears through me once again that I couldn't save my sister.

No, I need to push those thoughts out of my head. There are others involved, others who are hurt. I stand there, gaping at the last bed on the right. My family almost killed this woman.

THE WHOLE STORY

A lone visitor has his back to me: a son, a husband? I can't see his face, but dirt covers his raggedy clothes, and one of his toes sticks out of his shoe. The other foot doesn't have a shoe.

I trudge over to the bed. The man glances up at me apprehensively, as if he's expecting bad news. The curly ash blond hair is familiar, the blue eyes and square jaw.

The woman in the bed. Her features, despite the black and blue, are the same as his, and it hits me who this is.

"Nissa?" he says tentatively, confusion in his quiet voice. He stands, and I study his face as he scans my nurse's aide uniform. Basil.

I grip the railing on the side of the bed. His mum could still die—she's not out of the woods yet. This is so real, all these other victims among my family.

"I work here," I choke out, my head hanging. I can't look into his eyes. "I was here when they brought your mum in." And my sister. And my parents. I can't tell him that though, that my family's house crushed his home, demolishing his possessions and almost killing his mum. It's a miracle his mum lived.

I pull over a chair and slump down into the seat. How many days ago did we see each other at the market? Two weeks. Three. It feels like an eternity.

Giselle was there with me.

The room begins to close in around me again, and I take a few deep breaths and concentrate on Basil and his mum.

Micki said they lived in a poor neighborhood, but I never even noticed with Basil, his clothes or anything, that day. I guess I was too busy admiring those blue eyes and his long lashes. But I can tell now that his clothes were old and worn before he survived this disaster. And he's thin, not as gaunt as his mother, but he body is an unhealthy lean.

"How's she doing?" I barely manage.

He shrugs. "She's unconscious, and they don't know when she'll wake up, but at least she's alive."

Here's this man, sitting with his mum taking care of her. I have nobody to take care of anymore, nobody to take care of me.

I should've been home taking care of Giselle. If I had been, my body would be covered in a gray sheet like the rest of my family, but at least I wouldn't be filled with a numbing pain, one that'll maybe lessen one day, but will never go away.

The tears start again, and I wipe my cheeks. A stalk shouldn't tip over, shouldn't rip a hole open in the ground beneath my house.

But it did, and now my family is dead, and I don't know why.

Chapter Thirteen
Basil

Mumsy is quiet. The doctors don't know when she'll wake up, but she's alive, and my bruises and cuts will heal. They're nothing compared to her battered body.

The amazing girl across from me brushes her wet eyes. Nissa must have a heart of gold, to feel such anguish for someone she never met. I still can't get over that she's a nurse here, that I'm seeing her again. It must've been her in the park the other day.

The long room is jam-packed with beds. How I'd love to be in a quiet room alone, but we have no coin, and I can't exactly return to the forest to grab a bit of gold. It doesn't matter anyway 'cause Mumsy isn't aware of where she is.

"Are you here to take care of Mumsy?" I ask. So many nurses and doctors have been in and out that I don't think I've seen the same one twice.

"I'm a nurse's aide," she says softly.

I pretend to know what that means, but I'm not sure if she's really a nurse or not then.

"It's weird seeing you again. Thanks for your help at the market. I slipped that tomato in when she wasn't looking. It was good." It was actually the only one Mumsy didn't complain about.

Her lips quirk up in the corner, but it's more an acknowledgment and not a smile. I want to see her smile again.

"Basil Hagen?" A sheriff's deputy struts up to Mumsy's bed.

My muscles tense at the gruffness of his voice, but he can't know what I did. There was too much activity going on around our house, so I'm guessing nobody searched the woods and found my gold.

"Yes, sir?" I stand, but he waves me to take a seat and pulls over another chair.

"I should go," Nissa says as she pushes up from the chair.

I don't want her to go yet. She might work in this hospital, but there's a lot of people here, and who knows if I'll see her again. "Can you stay a bit longer?" I ask.

She looks to the deputy, who nods his assent, and she plops back down. She's holding a bitty stuffed bear in her hands. I hadn't noticed it until now.

THE WHOLE STORY

"I'm Deputy Dag Olsen, and I want to talk to you about what happened." He pauses for a moment, considering Nissa, before continuing. "Were you aware of the existence of this stalk in your yard?"

I shake my head. Better for them to think I'd never seen it. "It's a big yard, and I'm not out there much. Neither is Mumsy. She hardly goes outside to use the privy."

"None of your neighbors had seen it either. Can you tell me what you were doing when it fell?"

Nissa lets out a sob and hides her head. It's surprising how a girl who works at a hospital and deals with this kind of thing every day still has so many tears. She too soft and sweet. Maybe she could be the answer I'm looking for, if she can help Mumsy after getting out of the hospital. I can even pay her for the work now with that gold.

The deputy clears his throat, and I glance back to him. My story—I'd thought about what I'd tell them many times, practiced it in my head.

"I was out in the woods searching for pieces of wood... I like to whittle... and as I was coming out, I saw someone running across the backyard."

"A normie or giant?"

I furrow my brow to make it look like I'm considering the question hard. "You know, now that you say that, it probably was a giant. I wasn't that close, so I don't know, but he was tall."

"So it was a man?" The deputy writes something down on his pad of paper.

"Yes. A man—I mean, a big man." Best to direct suspicion that way. "Then I heard loud noises and saw the stalk falling, and I ran for cover 'cause stuff was flying everywhere."

Nissa's shoulders tighten, and I want to give her a squeeze, tell her Mumsy will be okay.

"That's it," I continue. "After the dust settled, I ran for the house and was digging for Mumsy. And then I end up here." They cleaned up my wounds, gave me a few stitches, and allowed me to see Mumsy.

"Did you see where the man went?"

"No, sir. There was too much going on." Keep it vague.

"And you hadn't noticed the stalk in your backyard?"

"No." I force a laugh. "It'd be hard not to have a giant stalk in my yard and not tell somebody about it."

He writes a few more notes down. "Nissa, may we speak to you again too please?"

Why would they want to speak to her?

"Um yeah." She stands abruptly. "Can we talk in another room?" Her voice is quiet, and I strain to hear

THE WHOLE STORY

her. The deputy nods, she gives me a quick look, and they disappear out the door before I can ask why they can't talk about it here.

Chapter Fourteen
Nissa

Deputy Olsen and I settle into a private room, and I steel myself for whatever he's about to say. My life is over as I know it, and I don't know what to do, or say, or how to act. The tears fill my eyes again, and the deputy hands me a tissue.

"Do you know Basil?" Deputy Olsen asks.

"No, not really." I met him, sort of, that day at the market with Giselle, when Mother made cookies and practically kicked her out of the kitchen. I'll never get to see my squirt with crumbs all over her face, or her excitement of finding a special treasure at the market. "Giselle and I were in the market, and Basil and I were at the same booth for a few minutes. Until Giselle took off."

I choke back a sob. My poor sweet sister is gone. I'll never get hugs and sloppy kisses, never read stories again, never …

THE WHOLE STORY

Mother, I need you. I squeeze Giselle's bear to give me strength because that's all I have now. Mother is gone just like Father. How did this happen? Why did this stalk destroy my family?

Deputy Olsen waits while I pull myself together. His eyes bore into me, like everyone else's will when they find out who I am. It's bad enough I lost my family, but now I'll have to deal with the guilt of the destruction their home caused. People will blame me, Basil will blame me, and I'm not sure I can take the hate.

"Constable Koch has arrived from Kjempeland," Deputy Olsen says, "and I can assure you we will work together to figure out what happened. I've called in a botany expert from the university to work with us too."

The stalks join our two worlds, and I've always seen them as safe, but now that peace is shattered. Every time I ride up a lyft, I'll think about my family, wonder if this stalk could rip apart the sky like the other one did.

"We need to clear away the debris so we can study the stalk to see why it collapsed. I'll make sure that any personal effects that can be salvaged will be set aside."

"Thank you," I sniff, knowing there'll be little that survived that fall. The only thing I have right now is Giselle's brown bear, and I'll never let that go.

I shuffle back to the room with Basil's mum and stop at the door to watch him. My brain is weary, and my body aches. Constable Koch showed up right before Deputy Olsen excused me, so I had to sit with him for a while. At least I know why my family is dead. My sweet sister was home sick, with my mum taking care of her. And Father came home at lunch to check on his baby girl… of course. He used to do the same thing for me.

Our house was the only one that fell through the hole. Dina's family was evacuated from theirs, although, as long as the whole doesn't spread, it won't fall through.

This whole event is unreal.

And yet, here I am, in the same situation as Basil, but I can't tell him the truth about me.

It's my family who fell on your house.

I hug the bear to my chest. I don't know how to say the words, how to tell him my family is the reason he no longer has a home, that his mum could still die.

My brain knows it's not my family's fault, that there's nothing they could've done to cause this tragedy, but if their house hadn't fallen, Basil's mum would be okay, and he'd be at home… he'd have a home. I should tell him the truth, but I can't.

He'll never forgive me, and right now I can't deal with that. I can't forgive myself for being away from my family. I should've been with them. I would've been

THE WHOLE STORY

taking care of Giselle if I hadn't been working today, and my body would be lying cold on a slab instead of my mother and father.

Right now that option seems preferable to living with this pain.

I have to do something for Basil. And if I admit it to myself, I'm doing it for me too. He's got no home, nothing, and I have an apartment I can share. A couch. I need to at least offer to him.

I shuffle over to his mum's bed and plunk down next to him. He gives me a sad smile, his eyes so dark and tired. I can't give him the truth yet, but I'll help him any other way I can.

"Do you need a place to stay? My apartment is not far away. I have a couch. It's not much, but…" It's a roof and a warm place to sleep, the least I can do.

We hardly know each other, and I'm willing to let him stay at my apartment. Maybe I'm foolish, but the guilt is too strong. My family is the reason he has nothing, I'm the reason he has nothing. It's a ridiculous notion. I wasn't there, and my family didn't want to fall to their deaths, but I'm the lone one left to bear the guilt.

Maybe I'm doing it for me. I don't want to be alone either, and the hard silence of my apartment will only become louder.

He looks as if he's about to say no, but then a yes pops out of his mouth. "I'd like that, thank you."

It'll be awkward, but I owe it to him, and I'll do what I can to make up for his loss. I hope he doesn't lose his mum as I did.

Chapter Fifteen
Basil

Sweet mother almighty. I'm going home with Nissa, the girl who I thought was too good for me. I'm sure I could stay at Denis' house, but I can't pass up this opportunity to get to know her better. Plus, she lives so much closer to the hospital than Denis does, and I can get here quickly if something happens to Mumsy.

I can't figure out why she'd invite me to stay with her though. Maybe she feels sorry for me, for losing my house and all, but when it comes down to it, we didn't lose much 'cause we didn't have much.

Nissa though. I thought she was a good girl, but she's inviting me back when she doesn't barely know me. It can't be about sex, not with all those tears she's shedding. Whatever her reason, I don't care.

I check in with the main nurse again, who assures me I can leave since there's nothing they can do for Mumsy, and we head down the hallway. Nissa's gripping that stuffed bear like she's afraid someone might steal it, and I want to ask about it, but feel like now isn't the time.

"Hey, man, are you okay?" Hands grab me and spin me around. Denis holds onto me, studies me with a concern he hasn't shown since I was younger. "I saw your house, or what's left of it. Those giants did a number on it. Can't believe you survived." He pulls me into a hug, and I let him. Circumstances allow for it at this time.

"I'm fine. Just some cuts and bruises." I clench my scratched-up hands. Lots of cuts and bruises actually from digging to get Mumsy out. They'll heal quickly though. "Mumsy's doing okay for now. She's not awake, but the doctors hope she'll come out of it. Maybe in a few days." At least she's here in the hospital. I feel bad about the three giants who died, but it was an accident. If that scary one hadn't threatened me and chased me down the stalk, none of this would've happened.

"I couldn't believe it when I saw it. Where the hell did that stalk come from? Did you know it was back there?" He blasts off his questions quickly, but before I can answer, he glances at Nissa. She's standing close enough to me I can feel the heat of her body. "Who's this?"

"Nissa. She works here. She offered me a couch to sleep on since the house is gone."

THE WHOLE STORY

Denis smiles at her, and she says hello quietly. I need to get her out of here. Or maybe it's that I want to get out of here, with her.

"I had no idea it was there, but um, we're worn out from the day. She's been working her taking care of everybody. I'm going to get some sleep, and I'll come talk to you in the morning."

"Gotcha. I'll talk to you tomorrow then. You know where to find me." He gives me a one-arm squeeze and takes off.

Nissa and I continue on, but we barely make it through the lobby when a group surrounds us. "Basil, Basil," they shout. "What happened? Tell us what you saw? How did the stalk tip over? Is your mum okay?" They shoot off question after question, even more than Denis.

I wave my hands at them. "Who the bloody hell are you?"

"Moorgan Daily," one guy blurts. I can't understand what the others say though, but I know who they are. The press.

This story is going to make the news.

I reach around to grab Nissa's hand for support, but she's nowhere to be seen. I scan the lobby but find nothing, so I turn back to the press people.

"I was looking for wood back in the woods…" I start my story, the same I told the deputy, but this time adding about how things were falling on my head as I tried to make my escape.

They eat up my story, act all happy to hear that Mumsy is okay even though they really don't care, and ask me how much I know about the giants, which is nothing.

I've never taken the lyfts to Kjempeland after all, and I've never met any giants—only seen them around here or there.

"And do you have a fund set up?" asks one of the reporters as the other questions start to dry up.

"Fund? For what?"

"For donations. Our readers want to know how they can help."

Crikeys. People will want to give me coin? This will tide me over until I can get to the gold coins again. It might be a good idea to stay away from the woods for a while.

The reporter gives me a name of somebody at the bank, a place I've never been before, and assures me that the woman there can help me.

Donations would help a lot to pay the hospital bills Mumsy will have. Maybe I can get a job while she's stuck in here.

THE WHOLE STORY

"I'll go talk to her first thing in the morning. Thanks."

The press crew leaves me alone, and minutes later Nissa shows.

"Sorry, I didn't feel like being asked a hundred questions." Her exhausted face looks how I feel, and I want to get back to her place.

"No problem. You ready to go?"

"Yes, let's go."

Chapter Sixteen
Nissa

Giselle never got the chance to stay with me. We could've had at least a few years where she would still fit in my bed. I used to be sad thinking that one day she'd be too big to stay with me, and now that won't happen anyway.

Ever.

I should go to Kjempeland to see my extended family, to start planning funeral arrangements, but I just want one night to myself before I'm surrounded by people who'll be asking questions I can't answer. The giants at home will grill me on what's going on, and the normies down here will grill me about my life and family if they find out who I am.

"Nice apartment," Basil says, staring around my space. It's small, but at least I have a bedroom.

"Are you hungry?" I ask him, realizing I never acknowledged his comment. Maybe this was a mistake; maybe I should've come back to my apartment alone.

THE WHOLE STORY

Alone with nothing but the bear.

"A bit." He looks at me as if he's unsure of what he should do.

"I'll be right back." I step into my room and straighten my pillows, giving Giselle's bear a good place to sleep. The emptiness spreads inside. I'm alone. I have no family. I have so little to remember them by, so little of my old life in Kjempeland, except my cozy blankets, the coffee pot in the kitchen, and a few other things.

I return to the other room.

"I'll get bread for sandwiches." I trudge over to the ice box and stare inside the door. There's no bread in there. "We can't have sandwiches. I'm out of bread."

"You keep it in your ice box?" Basil asks.

No. Of course not. I shake my head. My mind isn't on straight right now. I'm not sure it'll ever be on straight, not sure how I'll ever live with the sharp pain of loss in my chest.

"I can make sandwiches if you have that stuff. I make dinner for Mumsy all the time."

I glance at the bag in his hands.

"While you do that, would you like me to wash your clothes?" They gave him some extra clothes at the hospital, but they're too large. I'm sure he'd rather be in his own. "I need to scrub the blood out of mine anyway."

"Sure. Thanks."

SUZI WIELAND

I ask him to set a pot of water on the stove to boil and retreat to my bedroom. With the door shut, I perch on the edge of my bed and hug Giselle's bear in my arms, the tears wetting its fur. The beady black eyes stare back at me. He doesn't have a home either. He lost his home, the bed he slept on, the girl who took care of him and loved him. He has nothing except me, and I have nothing except him.

I take a deep breath of his fur, and the tears flood my eyes once again. He smells like Giselle, of little girl and innocence. I curl up on the bed and hold him tight to my chest. I should've never invited Basil back here. I can't keep crying because he'll wonder why I'm so upset, why I can't dry my tears.

I lie there for a while and gather my senses. He'll come looking for me soon. I should tell him I changed my mind and ask him to leave, but I can't. My family took away almost everything but his life, and I owe him.

By the time I return to the kitchen, the water is ready, and I carry the pot to the tub in the washroom. His clothes are filthy, with a few holes that will grow bigger with time. But it's all he has. We both have next to nothing, but I have an apartment. The idea provides scant solace though. I want my family.

I scrub at a stain on the front and feel something hard. My fingers wrap around a coin. A giant gold coin.

THE WHOLE STORY

He must've picked it up from the ground. My family's whole life rained down on him and his mum, and there's probably a ton of gold coins lying around.

I hold tight to the coin, unwilling to let go of one of the few connections I have left. It has to be from the jar of gold coins in the library. Mum had been bugging Father to bring them to the safe box at the bank, but he kept forgetting.

It belongs to me... to my family. But if I keep it, he'll wonder why.

It's not just the guilt I have over his life being destroyed, but it's the attention I'll get. If the normies know who I am, they'll never leave me alone. They might not all blame me—well, some will, but I'll always be *that girl*. Everyone will treat me differently, and I need all the normal I can get right now. I don't need pitiful looks, rooms that fall silent when I walk in, grimaces when they point out the girl whose family fell from the sky.

I set the coin on the counter and continue attacking that stain, and after hanging the wet clothes to dry, I take the coin and bring it out to the kitchen. Basil is setting the table with sandwiches and carrots.

I hold out the coin. "Is this yours? I mean I found this in your pocket. It's giant gold." Geez, can I be more obvious, interrogating him like a constable?

He plucks the coin from my hands and studies the front, then the back. "Giant gold, huh? I must've picked it up off the ground. Is it worth much?"

It's priceless... to me.

"Not much, I don't think. Can I keep it? It's kind of neat."

I'm awful. He's lost his home and all his possessions, and here I'm trying to take back a gold coin that could be used for new clothes or saved for when he needs to find a new place to live.

He stares down at the coin in his hand, flips it over a few times, but then his hand swings into the air, and the coin flies towards me. "Of course you can have it."

He doesn't know it, but his small gesture means more than anything.

Chapter Seventeen
Basil

Nissa doesn't know how much that coin is worth, but it's the least I can do with all she's doing for me. Besides, she seems so down, and I want to see her smile.

We eat in silence at her tiny table until the quiet gets to me.

"So, um, did you see that the newspaper people interviewed me?" I ask. She nods but says nothing. "It'll probably be in the newspaper tomorrow." Which means I should get to the bank and see if the lady can set me up with that account.

She stares off over my shoulder. "I don't understand how it could happen. How does a stalk fall down?"

"I'm sure it won't happen again. Like I told the deputy. I saw that giant running away with an axe in his hand. He probably cut it down."

Her brown eyes grow wide, and she opens her mouth but then purses her lips and doesn't speak for a few moments. "What did he look like? You said he was a giant?" The words rush out of her mouth.

The deputy had shown me the dead body, and I confirmed it was the person I saw. He's dead, so it's not like he'll be hurt by my lie. "Yeah, it must've been him who chopped down the stalk. He was big. Had red hair and a beard, and..."

Her face goes all pinched.

"I'm sure it won't happen again. It's never happened before, I mean. Did you want some more food?" I ask, trying to distract her. Maybe she's afraid of another stalk falling down. She shakes her head, so I clear away the dishes.

"I'll get a blanket out for you, and then I'm cleaning up and going to bed." She shuffles away, and my gaze falls down her back, from her shiny brown braids to her curvy hips. Her skirt is long, but I'm guessing she's hiding shapely legs underneath. She disappears into her room, and a few seconds later, returns with the blanket and pillow.

"Thanks." I take them and breathe in the fresh soap smell—Nissa's smell. She goes into the washroom and comes out shortly, clean and fresh in her nightgown that hangs down to the floor. I can't help but imagine what she looks like underneath. She's about the size and shape of Eva.

THE WHOLE STORY

Nissa says goodnight and gives me the washroom to clean up. It feels good to get the dirt off, but I swear I still smell like the hospital. Nissa's whole apartment, this washroom, is so much better than my old house.

I sprawl out on the couch and listen to the dead silence. I could open the window, but I don't move. Some small noises escape from across the wall. Her apartment might be nice, but the walls are paper thin like they are—were in my home. I'd swear she's crying, and hard.

I should go to her. But what if she wants to be alone?

The crying continues though, and I have to do something. She's helping me, and I should help her.

The door creaks when I swing it open, and I say her name.

"Yes," she replies in a strangled voice.

"Are you okay?"

"Yes," she says again. I don't deal with crying women often, so I have no idea what to say, especially 'cause I don't know why she's so upset. Just overwhelmed from the day maybe, seeing so many dead people at once.

I step over to her bed and huddle on the edge, put my hand on her shoulder. She sniffs.

"Why are you crying?" I ask.

"I just..." She stops, and I wait for her to talk, to get whatever's weighing her down off her chest.

"You're safe here. Nothing like that will probably ever happen again." I'm pretty sure of that, but I can't exactly explain why.

She sniffs hard again and sets her hand on top of mine. Ever so lightly she tugs on my arm, and I slip under the covers with her, putting my arm around her waist. Her body is warm against mine, and it wouldn't take long to get steamed up, but now is not the time.

Nissa's no Eva. She's the type of girl who wants to know a guy first. I'm okay with that. We'll get to know each other soon... I'm sure of it.

Chapter Eighteen
Nissa

I wake up and find myself in Basil's embrace. I hardly know this man, and I invited him into my bed. Even though he can't see me, my face heats up.

He was so sweet, comforting me last night, such a gentleman, unlike so many of the giants I've dated.

I don't want to get out of Basil's arms and start the day. I don't want to go up to Kjempeland and face hundreds of pitying faces. I don't want to figure out how life will continue without my family, but I have no choice.

The ironic thing is that he's trying to comfort me, and it sounds as if my father was responsible for the stalk falling. Why would he chop down a stalk though? He's smart enough to know what would happen, not that it'd rip a hole in our world, but that it'd fall and hurt the normies close by. Nothing about this is making sense. It was him though, the way Basil described him—his red hair and beard.

No, stop. Those thoughts are too much for me.

I set aside Giselle's bear, roll over, and study Basil's face as he sleeps. He's got a few freckles under his eyes and over the bridge of his nose. I almost reach out and touch the curls at the side of his face, rub my fingers over the scruff on his chin.

He's beautiful.

I will his eyes to open, but he's still sleeping. Maybe he didn't have a night full of fitful dreams like me.

He finally stirs. I should turn away, but I want to soak in his stunning blue eyes and those soft curls.

"Hey," he says, pushing a few loose strands of hair behind my ear. I've spent the night in his arms, but I'm suddenly aware of how close he is, how good he smells.

"Hey." I've only slept with two men in my life, back before I'd turned twenty. The guys were not quite full-sized, a bit younger than me, and even then it was awkward because of their height. I've always wondered about normie men but hadn't taken the leap yet. I'd just gone out on a date for the first time down here, wasn't even close to having sex with a normie, but I was curious about them... About Basil.

I shouldn't be thinking about what's under his clothes, but right now those thoughts fill the hollowness inside me, keep away the thoughts that my father could be responsible for my mother and sister's deaths.

THE WHOLE STORY

"I hope I didn't keep you awake," I say.

"No. I slept fine. This bed is better than anything I've ever slept in." He closes his eyes and sighs. "I'm not sure I even want to get out of bed. There's so much to do today though."

Like go to Kjempeland. The numbness washes over me again. I have three funerals to plan.

"Do you have to work today?" he asks, pulling his arm off, taking the warmth of his body with him.

"No." They told me to take as many days off as I needed, but I don't know how long that'll be yet.

Not only do I need to return to Kjempeland, but I'll have to check in with the deputy again. I don't know why Father would've come down the stalk when he was supposedly home from lunch to check on Giselle.

Maybe... hopefully, it was another giant.

"I have other things I need to do," I say. "I'll stop by and see your mum later too."

"Mumsy would like that." He closes his eyes and sinks back into the pillow. "I don't even know where to start. My house is gone, all my clothes."

All because of my father. The words hurt to even think about. "You're welcome to stay here for as long as you want. It was nice having company." I snuggle into him and give him a squeeze on the arm.

"I appreciate that, thank you." He leans over and kisses my forehead, and then he rolls out of bed. I watch his retreating figure, wishing he'd return, but it's too late.

This day has started, and I have to face it head on.

I pull myself out of bed and get the coffee pot out. It's large, but not giant-sized like so many other things from home. Giants drink stronger coffee, which means they drink less of it. It's still slightly bigger than the normie's pots though, so hopefully Basil won't notice.

"Do you want coffee?" I call, unsure if he can hear me from the washroom. He yells back no, which relieves me. Now I can make it as strong as I want.

I run my finger down the side, over a small dent in the copper. My special coffee pot. I'll never have morning coffee with my father, never see Giselle wrinkle her nose up when she takes a drink from Mother's cup.

The washroom door opens, and I blink away my tears. Basil can't see me crying.

Chapter Nineteen
Basil

Holy Schmoly. Nissa doesn't know what she was doing to me there in bed. Her massive jugs were calling to me, but I held back and just gave her a kiss. I had to get out of there 'cause my dong was about to rise. I've settled down now.

The bank should be open, so I need to get over there and stop by Denis' place and go see my home, and then Mumsy. Sweet mother almighty, I do have a lot to do today.

After making breakfast, I head to my neighborhood. It's a warzone with a bunch of people hustling around removing debris. The giant house landed on ours, and it's a miracle Mumsy made it out alive. I still can't believe that it's visible now, the brown stalk cutting a wide swath into the woods.

"Nasty, isn't it?" Adrian, my neighbor, huffs. "Me and the missus be thanking God it didn't smash us. I heard that crack and looked up to the sky." He rambles on for a while until I wander away. Adrian'll never shut up once he gets someone listening to him.

Several debris piles surround the house and the stalk. It'll take days for them to clear everything away.

I scan the site for someone who seems like they're in charge. I need to help, do what I can. It's my house after all.

"We have all the paperwork we need now, Mr. Hagen," the bank lady says.

"So everything will be taken care of from now on?" I rub my aching hands—I've never sighed my name so many times before. My choices were to have the donated coin released to me or have the bank handle the hospital bills. No question on the best way to do it.

I don't want to screw things up for Mumsy, and I also don't want the temptation of using the donated coin for myself.

The bank lady gives me a nod. "Thank you, Mr. Hagen." She shakes hands with me and brings me to the door. I've never had a bank account, and this is a new and exciting thing, even if it's not coin I'll be using for myself. Maybe when things settle down, and Mumsy is back home under the care of a nurse, I can finally get a job and have my own coin in the bank.

THE WHOLE STORY

That is if Mumsy will allow me to hire a nurse. Time to go see her and then go back to my house and help clean the mess again. There's so much to do.

At the hospital, I step inside the smelly room, but her bed is empty. My stomach rolls. Something happened to her last night while I was with Nissa. I should've stayed where with Mumsy.

"Oh, Mr. Hagen." A nurse stops by my side. "We transferred your mum to the fourth floor continuing care unit."

"She's alive?" The relief rolls through me.

"Yes. They can tell you what room she's in up there."

I thank her and make my way upstairs to the nurses' station, where they direct me to the room. It's not much different from the one downstairs.

Mumsy's frail body doesn't move when I touch her arm. "It's me, Basil. I, um..." This is so weird. "I'm okay. Our house isn't. But when you get out of here, I'll build a new house for you."

Even though I'm speaking quietly, I feel like I'm talking to this whole room. Nobody else is in here—no visitors, no nurses, but there's still a bunch of ears listening to me from those unconscious patients in bed.

Where is Nissa now? I can't wait to see her again. She smelled so pure, so fresh and clean. It's funny how I like that better than the other girls, ones like Eva and the girls from the BoomBoom who wear way too much stinky perfume.

Of course I want that sweet girl to wrap her legs around me so I can pound into her. She's quiet, but probably has a wild girl hidden inside.

Something clanks across the room, and I open my eyes. The nurse is going from bed to bed checking on patients. Time to go. I've got a few coins left. I'm going to pick up food and have dinner ready for Nissa when she returns.

That'll impress her.

Chapter Twenty
Nissa

Every bone in my body aches, every joint, yet I've done nothing but sit on my arse all day. I've received a lot of hugs, shed a lot of tears, and made arrangements for the funeral.

A triple funeral.

I've asked a lot of questions, and others have asked the same of me, and I kept to myself what Basil said about my father and the axe. I don't need them hating on him too, especially if we aren't sure what happened.

My mind is a bowl of mush, and I'm so done with talking.

At least my parents were smart and had their finances in order, and the accountant assured me there'd be coin left over after the funeral, maybe even enough to pay for a year's worth of school if I decide to go. It doesn't relieve me of any pain though.

Right now I can't make any decisions about the future. I probably wouldn't have been able to get the funerals planned if it wasn't for Dina's mum and my aunts.

I grip the railing in the lyft as I travel back down to Moorgan, unable to enjoy the pretty view. Some crazy person could attack a stalk at any time, bring another one down. Somebody who doesn't want giants in Moorgan.

The strange looks follow me out the door. Some giants knew me from before, when I was the mini-g who didn't fit in with the rest of them, but now they know me as the girl whose family fell to the ground.

At least down in Moorgan, I can blend in with everybody else.

The walk home takes me by the park I'd once brought Giselle to, but I know if I stop to sit on the bench to rest my weary feet, I'll just feel worse.

But I won't cry. My tears have been depleted, and the hole in my heart is spreading across my body. I have no energy left for crying even if I had the tears inside me.

I open the door to my apartment, ready to put my nightdress on and crawl into bed, but a wonderful smell stops me. Basil stands in my tiny kitchen, a spatula in hand. Bacon-wrapped steaks are frying on the stove, and he has a bottle of wine.

He did this for me.

"Hey," he says tentatively. I'm standing here staring at him, and I should answer, but I'm too overwhelmed.

THE WHOLE STORY

This whole day has been filled with people doing things for me, people who loved my parents and my sister, who love me, but here's this guy who doesn't even know me, and he cares too.

He wraps me in his arms and pulls me tight for a hug, and all I can smell is bacon grease.

"I hope you don't mind that I made you dinner. Are you hungry?" he asks as he steps away.

I want his embrace back to warm my chilled body.

"Yes, I'd love dinner." It's the last thing I want right now, but he did this for me. The potatoes are on the stove too, and a loaf of bread is already cut on the counter.

"Why don't you sit. I'll get everything dished up."

"I need to change first." My stiff scratchy dress binds me tight, but that's not why I want to change.

I close my door and snatch Giselle's bear off the bed. I watched my father and mother plan my grandparents' funerals years ago, but I never imagined how difficult it would be. I thought I'd be old when I buried my parents, and I never considered I'd be burying my sister.

I love you, squirt, I whisper to the bear, then put him back on my pillow. I almost step into the hallway but realize I never changed, so I find new clothes.

SUZI WIELAND

In a few minutes I have a plate of food and a glass of wine, and Basil settles across from me with a satisfied smile on his face. Before he can ask me about my day, I ask about his.

"Long," he sighs. "I saw Mumsy. She's about the same, but they moved her into continuing care. And I went out to my house. You should come see it with me. It's really smashed up bad. There's nothing left."

A sharp pain shoots through my chest, and I clench my teeth. The house I played in, my room and all the things I didn't have space for in Moorgan. There's nothing left of my family either.

He continues talking, but I can't listen because I'm trying hard to stay upright and look normal. He'll hate me if I tell him the truth, that it was my pop who chopped down the stalk. Had he come home at lunch and discovered it and then climbed down? Even if he did, what would possess him to chop it down?

Knowing what he did hurts so badly.

"What do you think?" Basil says, his blue eyes raised. I have no idea what he said.

"I'm sorry. About what?"

"I asked if you wanted to go see Mumsy with me tomorrow."

THE WHOLE STORY

"Of course. I'm sure she'd love the company." I can make things up to her son, but I'm not sure what I can do for her, so the least I can do is visit.

He smiles softly, as if he understands, and talks about his friend Denis. It's a safe subject, and I nod along at all the right places.

After dinner, we lounge on the couch. He's close, but not too close. I want to scoot over and put my head on his shoulder and close my eyes, but don't want to seem forward.

"Would you like me to rub your feet?" he asks.

Um, really? Is he serious? I have to do that for people in the hospital, rub their skin to keep their circulation going, move their legs, and it's not something I enjoy.

"I mean. I do it for Mumsy all the time. She has foot problems. Well, that's part of her problems. Why don't you lay down."

I slide to the end of the couch and put my feet into his lap. He strips off my socks and pushes my skirt up to my knees. His fingers are firm on my arch, and he seems to know exactly where to exert pressure.

"Did you go to school for this?" I laugh because it's hard to see Basil being a masseuse.

"No, but like I said, I do it for Mumsy."

"You're a good son." And I used to be a good daughter, but that's impossible now because my father chopped down a stalk.

"Thanks," he says, and we fall into a quiet lull. Not only does he knead my feet, but he runs his hand up and down my shins tenderly.

His caress clears away the chaos in my head, and I will my muscles relax, the tension in my shoulders that's turned into an ache. I want to put everything out of my head and enjoy his touch. I sneak a peek at him through my lashes. He's staring at me, a longing desire.

If his fingers make me feel so good, his kiss could fill the emptiness inside. It's temporary, but it's better than the miserable suffering.

I take his hand and slip it up my thigh, underneath my dress. I don't dare open my eyes because I can't bear to see if there is rejection on his face. But he slides closer to me and lifts my knee against his chest, my other leg lying to the side.

His hand wanders up my skin to my panties, and he runs his fingers along the edge, back and forth on my skin, over and over until finally his fingers slip underneath the thin fabric. His stroke is tentative at first but gains confidence. I sigh at the warmth flowing inside me and spread my legs the slightest bit wider. I want to forget everything. I only want to feel his touch.

THE WHOLE STORY

The pleasure from his hands takes the place of the pain. The bulge under his pants pushes into my leg, and a moan escapes my mouth. Then he's on me. His lips attack mine, his hands grapple under my shirt.

I want him, and now I know he wants me.

We fumble off our clothes, and his mouth is all over my lips, my neck, my breasts. His body is hot next to mine, and I spread my legs and pull him to me. He thrusts inside me, and I gasp. It's so much better than my previous times.

As he rocks into me, all I can think about is the good feelings inside me, and for a few moments I'm happy.

Chapter Twenty-One
Basil

I wake up again with my arms around this radiant woman, except this time she's naked. I run my hand between her legs, and she sighs contentedly, then flips over to face me.

"Good morning," I tell her. It's a wonderful morning.

She mumbles the same back and burrows into my chest. I'm smart enough to know not to push things with her. I'll wait until she makes the first move again. I sort of appreciate that anyway.

"Do you have to go into work?" I finger the thick braid hanging over her shoulder, wanting to unwind it. The shape of the braid is similar to the giant stalk, like she just took her hair and twisted it over and over until it was tight. I'm not sure how she did it so that they don't unravel on their own.

"No. I have today off," she says, her breath hot against my chest. I can't help it that the big boy gets hard.

THE WHOLE STORY

It doesn't take long for her to find it and get me riled up even more.

We roll around in the sheets again, getting hot and sticky, as lusty as it was last night—I love it.

When we finish, she lays her head on my chest and traces her finger around my belly button.

"Should we stay in bed all day long?" I ask. Or how about all week long?

"Maybe for the morning," she says quietly.

She's serious. I think she is at least.

I knew this good girl isn't so innocent.

We finally climb out of bed hours later. While I prepare lunch, she makes coffee with her old dented pot. Her movements are almost tender, ceremonial, but I don't say anything and watch her as I get our food. When I take a drink, I hide my grimace—too strong, way too strong.

We decide to go to the Riverwalk to hang out, which is fine by me. Just a short walk farther is the District, and maybe I'll bring Nissa there and show her how much fun dice is. Just a few games though. I'm changing my ways.

The area is fairly quiet, and we mostly stick to the trail along the river and stay away from the shops and touristy stuff. She's quiet, so I do most of the talking. I need to draw her out though.

"Do you come here a lot?" I ask.

"I've always loved this place," she says. "It's so peaceful away from the people."

Our shoulders keep bumping, and I get the urge to hold her hand. I should. She might like that.

"I haven't been down here all that much. I bet Mumsy would like it too." I reach out, entwine my fingers through hers, and she doesn't push me away.

"I wanted to bring my little sister down here, but I never got the chance. She would've loved getting her face painted." Her voice is still quiet, contemplative, and I strain to hear her.

I remember the sister now, that girl who bumped into her in the market. By the dour expression on her face, Nissa must not see her much. "Is she in town?"

Her grasp loosens, and she stares off into the river forlornly. "No, she's not around here." The tears gather in her eyes. She must miss her sister a lot.

"What kind of festivals do they have down here?" I ask. We flop down on the bench so close to the water, I can smell the mix of fish and boat engine exhaust in the air. Up the river on the other side are houses overlooking the water. I'd like to live in those one day, but that will never happen.

She talks for a bit about the different activities, and I'm actually listening. I want to learn about what she

THE WHOLE STORY

loves, the things that interest her. It's a new feeling for me.

I want to see her smile though, the girl I first saw at the market, the girl who knew Mumsy was being difficult.

"I think when Mumsy gets out of the hospital, maybe you can come shopping with us. She might take your advice this time."

"I doubt it." A small smile appears on her face, but the light doesn't reach her eyes. A heavy silence takes hold, and I'm not sure what to say.

"I bet you'll make a good nurse," I try. "The nurses at the hospital have been good to Mumsy. Do you like working there?"

"It's good." She doesn't offer any more, and I grit my teeth. I'm floundering. Maybe the Riverwalk just isn't the place to be now. Maybe somewhere else.

"I've got something I'd like to show you," I tell her, being all mysterious. "If you've got nothing you need to get back for." I leave it open so if she wants to head home, we can.

"I'm up for anything," she says with little enthusiasm. I'm not about to give up on her though.

"Have you ever played dice?" I ask, and she says no. "It's only the most fun game ever. Denis and I go to the District when we want to let off steam. It's addicting though. Once you start playing, it's hard to stop."

The neighborhood changes from wide open spaces to crowded buildings in need of repair. People hang on the street corners with nothing to do, except sell drugs, drink, or play dice.

We pass by a house of uptown girls, three of them loafing on the front porch in revealing clothes. Nissa watches them curiously as a guy strutting up the front steps holds his wallet open.

Another guy on the corner runs his eyes up and down her body, and she shrinks into me. I wrap my arm around her shoulders so that he doesn't get the wrong idea about her.

"Do you hang out here a lot?" Her head whips around, taking the sights in.

"Hang isn't the right word." Well, it is, but the way she said that made it sound like a bad thing. "We come down here to play dice, me and Denis. It's sorta our thing."

I lead her down a back alleyway to one of the dice places. A group of men kneels on the street with their dice, others standing behind watching.

"Basil," Einar calls, hopping to his feet. "Haven't seen you for a while. Where you been?"

Denis obviously hasn't been here; otherwise Einar would probably know what happened. He doesn't

THE WHOLE STORY

exactly read the newspapers though, and I don't need him to know how my house was crushed.

"I've been busy. This is Nissa." I move my arm down to her waist and pull her closer.

"Hey, Nissa." He drops his voice how he does with the ladies. "You come to have some fun? I can get you in the game."

Of course he can. He not only wants my coin but my girl too.

"We'll play a few games," I say. "Then we have dinner plans."

"Just a few?" One of the other guys scoffs. "You worried about going into debt with Einar again?" He laughs, and I give him a look to shut him up.

"Where's your boy today? Denis was telling me about that rum you had." Einar slaps me in the arm. "Where'd you get it? I want to get my hands on some."

The giant rum? Denis must've talked it up big if Einar's still wondering about it.

"He's probably still working. My neighbor gave the rum to me though. His brother was in from out of town and brought it. Don't know where it came from though, and he's gone."

"That's too bad." Einar frowns.

We drop down to the ground, and I explain the game to Nissa. We watch a few matches first, and then I let her play. She seems to be having fun, especially when she wins two games.

But then we lose three.

I pat my pocket. I need to leave enough coin for dinner. I want to take her somewhere nice.

"You ready to go?" I tug on her arm.

"Go?" Einar harrumphs. "You just got here."

Nissa almost looks like she wants to stay longer, but if we lose any more, I won't have any coin.

"Let's see," I say, pretending it's a big deal. "Hang out on the street with a bunch of stinking men, or go have dinner alone with a sweet lady? It's not much of a question." I wink at Nissa, and she blushes.

She takes my hand, and I pull her up.

"Catch ya later." I salute Einar and lead Nissa away. "What did you think about dice?"

"It's fun. I could see how it'd be easy to lose money quickly."

Way too easy. That's why Einar wanted me to stay. We talk as we wander down the sidewalk back into the better part of town, and when we reach the restaurant I want to eat at, I stop. "Want to go here?"

"Here?" She watches the couple going inside and peers into the window. "It looks expensive, Basil. I don't want you to waste your money."

THE WHOLE STORY

I wrap my arms around her waist so she's staring at me. "I'm not wasting it if it's for you." I've got that coin coming in for Mumsy's bills and the giant gold back in the woods. I can afford one nice dinner out. Just one dinner.

She gives me that appreciative look, the same one she does after sex, and I know there'll be no more argument from her.

The waiter leads us past a table filled with people dressed in nice clothes, people who can afford restaurants like this all the time. It's a life I want to live one day, and maybe if the donations pay for a special nurse to take care of Mumsy at home, then I can get a good job.

I'm not sure where we'll live—if we'll rebuild our home. It's one of many decisions I'll need to make soon. I don't want to think about all that now when I'm with this sweet girl.

I know what I want so I just watch Nissa. It's so cute the way her mouth purses as she stares at the menu with those big brown eyes. A guy passing by gives her a long look, which she doesn't notice, and the pride about bursts out. I'm with this special girl, and things are going well.

It makes me nervous and happy at the same time.

SUZI WIELAND

Dinner passes quickly, and I share some of the best stories of me and Denis' wins at dice, stories where Einar or the others thought they were going to walk away with our coin. She laughs along at their stupidity.

During dessert, I tell Nissa a funny story about Mumsy, but she stares off over my shoulder, a frown on her face. I stop talking and look behind me, not noticing anything weird, but then the conversation at the table over hits me.

"They should prosecute those damn giants," growls the one man.

"Like that'll ever happen. Our lily-livered council never stands up to those brutes." The second guy harrumphs. "How many stalks have to fall before they realize the danger?"

They continue to talk about the giants. Nissa's face is frozen, her eyes wide, but then her face droops, and her head falls. Those men are making it sound like it's the giants' fault the stalk fell. I've heard so many other theories from people, but I mostly ignore them. Those men shouldn't be blaming the giants though—it's not their fault the stalk fell. It's mine.

For a short time we got away from everything that was happening: Mumsy's injuries and those poor giants who died, but these men have brought everything back with their stupid talk and ruined our dinner.

THE WHOLE STORY

Our dessert is mostly gone, so I give the waiter a wave to get our bill. "How about we get going?" I say, hoping I can bring Nissa's smile back again once we get out of here.

Out on the sidewalk she's quiet, and I just feel like I need to apologize for what happened.

"I'm sorry you had to hear that. I was trying to have a nice time."

"They always blame the giants. For everything. I've even heard people complain that it's the giant's fault when it rains."

I laugh at the absurdity. Even I'm not that dumb. "Those are just stupid people."

"But if it was…" Her voice chokes off. "If it was that red-headed giant who chopped down the stalk and made it fall…"

I'm not sure why she's so upset about the giants. It's not like she knows any, at least not that I'm aware of, but she probably can't get the picture out of her head of the dead giants at the hospital. Maybe she's worried that it isn't a giant who chopped down the stalk and that somebody might try that again.

"I'm sure this won't happen again. The guy who did it is gone, so you don't have to worry."

Her head is down again, and her braids are covering her face, but I can hear her sniff. Maybe I can cheer her up with a gift, maybe some beautiful flowers. I know there's shops on the way home.

That'll do it I bet.

Chapter Twenty-Two
Nissa

A week has passed since I lost everything. A triple funeral, lots of talking to the constable and sheriff, and so many questions with no answers. Questions that may never be answered.

Only two things keep me going: Basil and my job.

I get through the day by working, unable to hide out at home anymore. Basil spends his days at his former house clearing away debris and preparing the site for a new home the neighbors want to help build. I haven't been able to go there even though he's asked multiple times. I can't see the fallen stalk that hasn't fully been removed, nor the hole in the sky.

It's break time now, so I run upstairs to see his mum, whose condition has not changed at all. She has become my confessional, and I tell her all the things I can't tell him, about my mother and father and Giselle. If she wakes up one day and remembers everything, I'll have to own up to the truth about who I am, but from listening to the doctors, I'm not sure that'll ever happen.

Basil chooses to ignore what the nurses are saying, believing that his mum will leave the hospital alive and well, and I don't have the heart to make him see the truth. The one time the nurse brought up the subject of letting his mum go, he got pretty mad. She wouldn't be alive though if she wasn't getting nutrients from a tube, but he isn't ready to give up on her yet. And neither am I.

I spill my secrets over my fifteen-minute break, tell her of all the tears flowing at the funeral despite the uplifting songs and wonderful words about my family. Tell her about her son and how even though he doesn't know it, he helps me get out of bed each day and face the world.

The afternoon passes quickly, and as I'm about to walk out the door, Deputy Olsen ambles in. I've been waiting for an update from him, and twice I almost went down to the sheriff station, so I'm glad he showed up here.

"Nissa." He gives me a nod with such a serious face. "Can we talk?"

We find an unused room and take a seat. I can't read him.

"I've been working closely with Constable Koch, and as you know, the site has been cleared of much of

THE WHOLE STORY

the debris, and we've been examining the stalk. As we first presumed, it appears to have been cut. Somebody deliberately chopped it down."

I suck in a hard breath. I tried telling myself Basil wasn't right, but now we have proof. My father is responsible. No other giant bodies were found, and he was seen with the axe.

"It was the man with the axe, just like Basil said." My father was a good man, and I don't know why he'd chop down the stalk.

"Axe?" He leans forward, rubbing his chin. "Basil saw a man with an axe?"

Doesn't he remember? He was there when Basil mentioned it. I try to remember that day in the hospital, but everything is a blur.

"Yes, he saw a man with an axe." I don't want to connect the dots for the deputy; I don't want to hear him say it was my pop.

"Not to me. He witnessed a man running away."

"I know he told me that because..." Admitting this next part kills me, and I feel like a traitor. "I remember what he said because he said the man had a red beard and that's my... my pop."

"No. It couldn't be your father. If a giant had cut it, the break would've been higher off the ground. Not to mention, he wasn't wearing shoes. He wouldn't climb down the stalk in bare feet and then chop it down. At least we can't imagine he would do that. The point is, we don't believe it was a giant."

"Oh, thank goodness." The relief swells inside me. It wasn't Father. But that means the responsible person is roaming around free. But is it a human or a giant who wanted to make it look like a human did it.

Deputy Olsen folds his hands and gives me a sour look. "I think I need to talk to Basil again."

"I'm sure he's out at the site. He's been there helping." I glance at the clock. "Oh, he might be home now. Usually he gets home after me." I've caught him in the shower multiple times and joined him. Not that the deputy needs to know that.

Deputy Olsen stares at me funny, and my face blazes.

"He's staying with you?" His brows furrow.

"He needed a place to stay." The guilt over his loss is still strong, but it's morphed into more. I need him to chase away the loneliness and pain. I need him to fill the silence when it becomes too overwhelming. I need him to make me forget if even for a short time.

"Let's go then." He escorts me out to the street, waiting until we're outside the hospital before speaking again. "We recovered anything that was salvageable, which is the other reason I needed to talk to you and

THE WHOLE STORY

Basil. Unfortunately, looters snatched some things, but—"

"People stole things?" A tragedy brings out the best in some, the worst in others. It shouldn't surprise me.

He smiles sadly. "Maybe the two of you can look through the items and claim what's yours."

I freeze, my blood running cold. No, Basil still doesn't know who I am. My father might not be responsible for what happened, but I've been lying to him all this time. If he finds out the truth, he won't want to see me, and then I'll be alone. The silence and emptiness of my apartment will match that of my cold heart.

"Can I ask you a favor?" Please, please let this work. "I know you probably think this is strange, that Basil's staying with me, but I owe him. My house fell on his, almost killed his mum. He knows it, and I know it, but we don't talk about it. I think it's easier for him to think of me as some random girl he once met in the market and ran into again at the hospital. The two of us brought together by tragedy."

He stares at me, lips in a thin line, but I don't need his approval. I just need him to go along with my request.

"It's hard," I continue. "People down here are mad at the giants, as if it's our fault my parents' house fell. And I know even now when the truth comes out, there'll still be people who blame us. And I want people to treat me like a normal person."

I've heard the angry talk in the market and on the streets, and I feel lousy for not defending my people, but I can't add to the huge load hanging over me.

"Can you please not talk about my involvement? I don't want to give him that reminder of who I am. It's hard enough with his mum being so close to death."

"I understand." He nods his assent, but I'm not sure if he does. At least he won't tell Basil who I am. Besides, Basil doesn't need any more stress in his life. I've already noticed the extra wine bottles. We usually have a drink at dinner, but there are way more bottles in the garbage than what we drink. He doesn't act like a drunkard though, so I won't say anything.

He needs his wine to get through the day, and I need him. And if he has his secrets, then I won't feel so guilty about having mine.

Chapter Twenty-Three
Basil

Dinner is almost ready, and Nissa should be home soon, so the knock at the door startles me. I open it up to find Deputy Olsen.

"Good evening, Basil. I was hoping to find you here."

Nissa must have told him I was here, or else he's a good detective.

I show him to the couch so he can update me on the investigation. Nobody has gone into the woods, so I feel safe that they haven't found my buried axe. The whole thing was a mistake, and I wish I could go back and make the decision to stay away from that house, but I can't. What's done is done.

He folds his hand and stares at me. "I know you've claimed some of your things, but we have a pile of the other stuff we recovered. Why don't you go down to the shop to get what's yours. The rest we'll return to Kjempeland."

There's probably some valuable items there, but I can't take it. Those things belong to the giants who died, and maybe they have family who want it. Maybe I should return that gold, but I don't have any explanation of where it came from. Maybe a few coins, but the volunteers have been keeping track of the things they find, and a small stash of gold suddenly appearing wouldn't be easily explained away.

"What about the beanstalk?" They took out the chunk where I'd chopped it, but the rest is still lying there in my yard and in the woods too. It took out quite a few trees when it fell, and some damage was caused to a few other houses in the woods, but luckily nowhere close to my hideaway.

"It's yours to do what you want, the part on your property at least."

Beanstalks make great firewood, but it'll take me years to use it all.

"So I can give it away or something?"

"Whatever you want."

That's what I'll do. There's so many people in our neighborhood who could benefit from the wood, and that'd be a simple way to get rid of it.

Deputy Olsen leans back into the couch and rubs his chin, his eyes narrowing on me. "The other thing I

THE WHOLE STORY

wanted to ask you about again was this man you saw leaving the site."

The way he asks the question puts me on edge, as if he thinks something is wrong. "What about him?"

"Can you describe him for me?"

I shrug, trying to pretend it's no big deal. "He had red hair and a beard. I thought it was a giant, but I'm not so sure now."

"Hmmm." The deputy nods. "And was he carrying anything?"

"Oh, the axe. Yeah. Did he cut down the stalk?" My palms are sweating, and I wipe them on my pants. I've got to calm down.

"That's the only proper conclusion, isn't it?" His dark eyes study me, and I shift in my seat and tug at the tight collar on my shirt.

"He must have. I mean, why else would he have an axe with him? Did you find it?"

"No, we haven't."

"He must be long gone then." I picture a couple of our neighbors. "Oh wait, there's this guy who lives down the street a ways. He's got red hair. Maybe you should talk to him. Those unruly kids of his are always running around our street getting into trouble. I've had to yell at them to shape up several times."

"You think it's him?"

Okay, I have to be careful here. I'd better not accuse a specific person. "No… I don't know. I don't know him that well." I don't know any of our neighbors well.

"I'll check him out." He stares at me for a moment before speaking again. "And you've never had a run-in with any giants?"

"Run-in?" I laugh. "I've never seen a giant in our neighborhood, and I've never even gotten close to the lyft. That's the only way up as far as I know, right?"

"Right. Other than a hidden stalk." His eyes bore right through me.

"Are there lots of these stalks across the city? I've never heard of them before." Why is he grilling me?

"There are a few recorded stalks, but they're on private property, and the owners don't want to bring attention to them lest they have thrill seekers coming to climb them."

We really needed to wrap this up, but I can't ask him to leave without sounding suspicious. "How do you climb a stalk?"

"It's actually fairly easy." He slaps his thigh with his palms, and I jump. Then he stands. "That's it for now. Make sure you get over to the warehouse in the next few days so we can return what's left to Kjempeland."

"I will."

THE WHOLE STORY

I take him to the door, and as soon as he's gone, I swill down the last half of that bottle of wine, wrap it up in a rag, and hide it in the garbage can. Then I open another bottle of the same wine.

Dang deputy.

The next morning, Nissa's still sleeping, a peaceful look on her face and that bear in her arms. I'm itching to go check out the things the deputy recovered from our homes, but last night she said she wanted to do something different on her day off, so I'll wait.

I can't help but tease her awake, tickling her jugs until she smiles. After we're done getting busy, I take in her content face—that's what I like to see. Her eyes are closed, and she has a small smile, but inside I know she's fully satisfied. She always is.

"Where do you go, Basil? When you want to get away?" She opens her eyes, and her smile widens.

I know what she means, but I also know an answer she'll love to here. "Your bed."

She laughs, just as I expect, but then her face falls serious. "No, I mean it. Where do you go when you want to get away?"

Her place is the Riverwalk, and mine... there's only one place that's special to me. "The woods."

She props herself up, raising her brows. "The woods?"

"Behind the house. There wasn't a lot of room in our house. I didn't even have my own bedroom. And I'd go back to the woods to be alone. And it's often where Denis and I went. He's got a hundred brothers and sisters."

"Will you take me there? I want to see the place that's special to you."

"Yeah." Denis and I carved out that area of the woods years ago, our private getaway.

Nissa pops up out of bed. "Let's go. I'm in the mood for adventure. Maybe we can have a picnic in the woods too. Let's make a lunch to bring along."

She's so irresistible, her round brown eyes and soft lips, her smooth dark skin. I can't help but think about sneaking off to the woods with her, hiding under a blanket with her, getting busy with her.

"Nope. We'll pick up some food at the market."

"That's so expensive." She's standing next to the bed naked, her jugs practically calling to me.

"Don't worry about it. I'm treating you." I retrieved another piece of giant gold earlier and converted it to our coin. I reach up and touch the purple nub on one of her jugs. The big boy springs to life again, and I adjust the blanket so she can't help but notice my stiffie.

THE WHOLE STORY

"Basil," she giggles. I grab her hand and tug her back into bed.

"One more time," I whisper into her ear and pull her onto me.

I didn't think this out very well. Then again, Nissa was the one who wanted to come here.

She stares at the piles of wood dotting the site of my old house. It's a mix of the giant home and mine. Well, mostly giant. The stalk seems even bigger when it's lying on the ground, and I look towards where it fell onto the woods. I'm not even sure how far back it goes.

Nissa shuffles over to a pile and slowly circles it, tears in her eyes.

"You okay?" I ask.

"Three people died here," she says in a quiet voice. Her lip trembles, and she slams her eyes shut.

For the first time it hits me. They're not just giants, they're people. They probably had families and friends who loved them, who are missing them now, and I am responsible for their deaths. It was an accident—I never meant for them to die, but it is *my* fault. Every time I climbed that stalk, I told myself it was for Mumsy, but I used so much of that giant gold on myself, thought it would never disappear.

I was so selfish.

If she ever finds out, she'll never forgive me. I'm glad her eyes are closed 'cause if she looks at me right now, she'd see my guilt.

I turn around and tug on her hand so we can head to the woods. She pulls away and steps over what appears to be a broken door. I can only imagine what's going on inside her head. She's seeing the house and the people who live there. I can't do that 'cause the guilt might explode inside my head. It was an accident.

"Let's go back to the woods." I squeeze her hand.

The comforting smell of pine gets stronger as we step into the silent trees. The land back here doesn't actually belong to us, and I don't know who the real owners are, but I've never seen anybody out here in all the years we lived here.

I pluck one of the wildflowers from a clump off to the side and hand it to her. She smells the sweet aroma and puts it behind her ear.

The well-worn path leads us to the spot, and Nissa laughs. "You have chairs out here?"

Chairs are a nice word for the crude seating. Years ago, Denis and I nailed together logs, spending hours scraping the bark away so we wouldn't scratch our arses.

"Ladies, first." I sweep my hand as if it's a grand gesture, and she smiles again—the light is missing from

THE WHOLE STORY

her eyes though. She takes my chair, but scoots to the end and pats the seat for me to sit. I plop my arse down beside her.

"It's peaceful out here. I can see why you come." She stares off towards the edge of the woods. It used to be my peace, but now my hidden giant gold reminds me of those who lost their lives. "What do you do when you're out here?" she asks.

Drink.

An empty bottle of whiskey lays within reach. If I'd known we were coming out, I would've hidden it away. I glance at the spot with my hidden treasure—totally unnoticeable.

Nissa squeezes my arm, waiting for an answer.

"Think about life. Where I want to go someday. Denis and I play cards and dice." And drink.

Way too much.

"What's in the box?" She points to a wooden crate in the corner that holds another bottle of liquor and the pink polka dot brassiere. I also stored a couple gold coins on the bottom of the box 'cause I didn't want to keep the giant gold in one spot.

"Nothing right now. Maybe you can give me something of yours to put in it."

"I'll do that."

She rests her head on my shoulder, and we loaf for the next hour talking about life and all the things we love until it's time to pull out the food from the market. I spread out a blanket, and we set out our meal.

"I have an idea for later," I say in between bites. "Let's go shopping."

"Shopping?" She tilts her head and raises her brows at me. The flower falls from behind her ear, and she puts it back. I want to do something special for her. She's done so much for me.

"I want to buy you a thank you gift." A vase, to hold flowers. She always brightens when I give her a flower, and there's plenty of places around her apartment that I can pick them from.

"You don't need to do that. I don't need anything." She smiles shyly. "Besides, you shouldn't be spending money on me. I know things are tight right now."

"But they're not. People are donating coin to the bank for Mumsy." All that coin is going towards Mumsy's care, but I can't explain to her how I've got a pot of giant gold in the woods.

"But that's—" She frowns. "Maybe you should use that money on your mum."

"I am, but there's leftover after paying those bills. And it's okay if I buy you a small token of appreciation. Nothing extravagant, I promise."

THE WHOLE STORY

I wish I could take those words back 'cause she doesn't seem to approve of me using the donations. She's right, but the stupid thing is I'm not using them for anything but Mumsy's doctor bills, and I don't know why I implied I was.

"You're too sweet." She kisses me hard, her hands roaming up and down my back. Maybe that idea about getting busy in the woods might come true.

Chapter Twenty-Four
Nissa

"You just missed Basil," the nurse says as I slip in to see Mumsy on my break. I will the nurse to leave so I can talk freely, but she's fiddling with the guy in the bed next to us.

Basil is so sweet, and seeing a hidden part of him that other day in the woods was special, especially hearing about his life and how he grew up. Until then, he hadn't talked much about himself, not anything serious, but then again neither do I. He's the only thing in my life keeping me sane. When I'm with him, I don't think about the pain of losing my family, at least not as much.

I glance at the guy across from me. "How long has he been here?"

"Three months." The nurse sighs and pats him on the arm. "The family isn't willing to let him go even though he has no chance of waking up."

THE WHOLE STORY

Like Mumsy. *I'm sorry,* I say silently, an apology from my family. It's not their fault, but I can't get rid of the guilt.

"The daughter visits every day though. It's a lot more than some of these other poor folk."

"It must be expensive. How do the families pay for it?"

"I know his family has coin, but others…" She glances at Mumsy. "The hospital pays for them when the family is destitute."

She can't mean Mumsy. Basil said he was paying the bills with the donations. "Are they paying for Basil's mum?"

I don't want to hear the answer. Things are not adding up with him. That vase he bought me yesterday was way more expensive than anything I needed, and he used the money people donated to him.

"Only at first. He's paying for it now. But there are four others in here who have nothing."

Okay, so he didn't lie to me. But still, he drinks too much, and I'm wondering how much time he spends gambling down at the District.

I survey the room full of patients. "That's wonderful the hospital takes care of these people. It makes me proud to work at such a facility."

"Yes, the administration does treat patients well here. It's not the same at other places."

The nurse finally completes her work and moves onto another patient down the room.

It hits me then. Basil said he hadn't been working before the stalk collapsed because of his mother, but he hasn't mentioned getting a job now either, and he needs to rebuild his house and replace the things he's lost. He shouldn't just use the donations; he should be doing things to better himself too.

It's not just him spending the donated money though, there are other things that I've been choosing to ignore. The wine. I see the bottles in the garbage, but we're not drinking all that together. He might not be the man I think he is.

I pull myself together, and at the end of the break, ask Micki if I can have the afternoon off tomorrow. I need to check on a few things, see what he's actually doing during the day, see if he's helping clean the site like he says he is.

I sure hope he is because I need him, and I'm not ready to let him go.

Chapter Twenty-Five
Basil

The doctor wants to see me today, to give me an update on Mumsy. I give Nissa a smile and a wave when I see her down the hospital hall. The circles under her eyes seem even deeper today, the lines in her face darker, but she waves back.

The doctor is waiting for me when I get there, and I plop down in the chair in front of his desk.

"I wanted to talk to you about your mother again. We've discussed this before, but I want to stress that we don't believe she'll ever come out of this state. She'll live the rest of her life in the bed. It's not fair to keep her here with us."

"But there's still a chance. I mean, she could still wake up, right?" Even in my ears my words sound rushed, desperate. Mumsy has to be okay. "I can bring her home, hire a nurse to help take care of her. I can afford it." The giant gold, I can use that. And maybe Nissa will help me. She'd be wonderful for Mumsy.

The doctor sighs, long and hard. "Mr. Hagen, she is not going to wake up. The only thing keeping her alive is what we're doing for her. The most compassionate thing is to let her go."

Let her go. I shrink down in my chair, a large rock expanding low in my belly, growing and tightening. I close my eyes. He wants me to kill her.

But I already killed her. If I hadn't gone up the stalk, none of this would've happened. I wouldn't know Nissa, but Mumsy wouldn't be lying in a hospital bed waiting to die.

Not one, not two, not three… but four deaths are on my head. I didn't want any of them, but does that matter? I'm still responsible.

"Mr. Hagen." The doctor's voice is tentative.

"I'm not ready to give up. It's my decision, right?"

"Yes, it is."

"Then not yet."

I need to clear my head, so I go buy a bottle of whiskey and retreat to the woods. I'm not ready for Mumsy to die, and I can't let Nissa know I'm responsible for ending four lives.

The whiskey burns as it slides down to my gut. I want it to numb the pain, but that shame won't go away.

THE WHOLE STORY

Four people are gone 'cause of me.

I crawl on the ground, the twigs and rocks digging into my skin, and swish away the leaves from my hidden spot. Inside is the box with the gold. I take out the small plastic case on top. *N and G* it says on the back. Must be the husband and wife.

I can't return it 'cause there's nobody to return it to. Their lives are done, but mine isn't. And as much as I don't want to admit it, Mumsy's is too. Maybe I should let her go, as hard as that'll be. Maybe the doctor is right that she'll never wake up. If Mumsy is gone, then I'll need to go on with my life. I've been ready to grow up for years, but she's refused to let me go. And now it's my choice to let her go. I don't want to, but I need to, she needs me to.

I'll make some changes, a lot of changes. A good job, no more dice, give the giant gold to someone who really needs it. I can be the man Nissa deserves.

The whiskey bottle lies on its side next to me. This is the first place to start. I remove the cap and take one final drink.

Then I dump the rest of the bottle and watch it soak into the black ground.

Chapter Twenty-Six
Nissa

Basil is drinking whiskey alone in the woods. At least that's better than gambling away other people's money down at the District. The vase, the flowers, the wine, the food. He has no way to pay for those things without using the donation money.

He's not the man I thought he was. He's a liar and a thief, and it doesn't matter that those people are donating the money to him. He has no right to spend it on himself... on me, on such frivolous things.

I need to kick him out of my place, but that will leave me alone. The godforsaken pit inside me will grow without him. Basil and work keep the torment at bay, and I'm not sure I can handle it alone.

But I can't let him stay either.

I hate him for doing this to me. Now I have to see him in his true light, and I'm not sure I'm strong enough to let him go. I used to think I was strong, but I was wrong. It wasn't me; it was my parents and family

THE WHOLE STORY

standing behind me that made me strong. Now I have nothing.

I hide behind the trees, waiting for him to go. He sits quietly for a while but finally leaves. I give it another ten minutes and creep into his home away from home, his safe place. Several empty liquor bottles litter the wet ground.

I need to follow him more, to see if he's helping with the mess in his yard. He returns home smelling of sweat and stained with dirt, but maybe he was in the woods drinking, watching everybody else work. I should ask the people out there.

Right before he left, he glanced into that box in the corner. And it had seemed as if he was looking at something in the ground too. I couldn't tell.

First the box.

The lid creaks as I raise it, and the bile rises up my throat. It can't be. I lift the giant brassiere out. Pink with black polka dots. Just like the one Dina described.

It was Basil. He was at her house. My stomach threatens to spill my last meal over the black ground, the answers right in front of me that I don't want to confront. He was in Dina's house, touching her private things, and he stole her gold.

I shared my bed with this man, with this pervert. How dare he break into someone's home and steal something so personal. He also took a bag of gold, but nothing else is in this box. I scan the site around me.

At the side of the clearing is an area that looks purposefully messy with leaves and a pile of dirt.

I drop to my knees and brush the dirt away to find a wood plank hiding a canvas sack. My fingers tremble as I carefully unzip the bag and reach inside, and my hand hits the coolness of gold coins. I rip open the bag.

A plastic case falls onto the ground. My pulse races as I reach for it, my eyes blurring.

No. I squeeze my eyes shut. No, please no.

I flip the case over to see the letters written on the backside. N and G. He was in my house. He stole things from Dina's house and my house. He was at the site right after the stalk collapsed.

He knew the stalk was cut with an axe.

I collapse on the ground, the sobs wracking my body.

Basil killed my family.

Chapter Twenty-Seven
Basil

I dump the rest of the wine bottle down the drain so I'm not tempted. Nissa isn't home yet, so now's the time to get rid of it.

Crikeys. She's probably going to notice that I stopped drinking wine. But I can tell her this bottle spilled and then make it sound like I'm trying to save coin and can't buy any more.

The weight on my shoulders deepens under these new lies. I can't do it. I need to tell her the truth, as much as I can, but she might not want me around anymore, and I need her.

All my buddies will laugh at me if I told them I'd stopped drinking. Well, all except Denis—he'll understand. But even so, right now I can't afford to be around any alcohol, and that means less time with my friends.

And it's why I need Nissa more than ever.

SUZI WIELAND

I need my mum too, but she's never coming back, hasn't been there for me for years. I toss the empty bottle into the trash and head out to the hospital.

Mumsy is still under her blanket, her body warm and breathing, but she's not alive inside. The doctors said it, and they've been saying it, but I didn't want to admit it.

The nurse is bustling around the room, and I squeeze by people standing around another patient to get to Mumsy.

Her hand is dry, her skin translucent, like it might dissolve at any point. She's my mother, and I don't want to let her go. Her life was hard, but we were okay until she had her accident. She gave up on life and became bitter.

I don't want that to happen to me.

I can't.

The nurse glances over at me and gives me a small smile. I know it's time to let Mumsy go so she can be at peace.

The doctors are happy. The nurses are happy.

Happy isn't the right word. Relieved maybe. They've known all along the best thing for Mumsy, but I couldn't see it. I do now.

THE WHOLE STORY

They'll remove her feeding tube and stop giving her the medicines. Her body is weak, so they don't think it'll be long. At least that gives me time to say goodbye.

I have so much to share with Nissa, and I hope it won't overwhelm her. My drinking, my mum. She's told me that she agrees with the nurses and doctors, so she'll be proud of me for my decision.

I hope.

She's not at home when I get back, and so I wait on the bed where I feel closer to her. The brown bear rests on the pillow like it does all day long, and all night it sleeps in her arms. I run my finger over its worn fur. Maybe I should buy her a new one.

But no. She's twenty-two years old and clutches to this bear like it's the most important thing in her world. Maybe I can get it a companion, not a bear 'cause I want to do something different. Maybe a cat or a dog.

That's what I'll do when I have free time, and then her bear won't seem so lonely anymore.

Chapter Twenty-Eight
Nissa

I still haven't been back to where my old house used to sit. I can't bear to see the place where we once lived, where we were so happy. And I won't see it on this trip up to Kjempeland this time either. My head is down so they can't see my wet face and red eyes as I shuffle down the sidewalks of my former world.

Life goes on for everybody but me. Nobody else here lost their mother, their father, their little sister. They care about me, they worry for me, but I'm down below where I need to be.

There's nothing left for me up here.

The trees shade the sun from my eyes, and I step onto the trim grass. The giant cemeteries are one of the few places that actually look similar to their counterparts in Moorgan. The bodies are spaced wider apart, but the gravestones are not any larger than the normies.

My knees sink into the fresh dirt as I kneel down in front of Giselle's stone. My fingers trace her name.

THE WHOLE STORY

Giselle Lund. She'd complain about her stone if she could see it right now. She'd only been to a few funerals in her short life, but she questioned why the gravestones weren't bright colors like our homes. *Why are they black and brown? That's so boring.*

I would've ordered her a bright yellow one if it had been available.

"I love you, squirt." A wave of tears cascade down my face. I thought I'd been done crying, but I haven't been able to stop since I found out about Basil. His betrayal is too much.

Don't you ever cry over a boy. He's not worthy of your tears.

Mother's words repeat in my head as I stare at her grave, seeing her beautiful face. She meant those stupid boys that hurt me when I was a girl, the ones who wouldn't date me because I was a mini-g, the ones who made fun of me. No matter how many times she told me, I still cried.

But I can't now. I won't anymore.

I'll never find love with a giant, and neither will I with a normie. The normies won't understand my world, they won't understand my loss, and I'll experience disappointment after disappointment with them.

I talk to my baby sister, telling her the stories Father used to tell us. When I'm done, I move on to my father and mother, apologizing for the stupid mistakes I've made, the trouble I caused for them.

I won't make those mistakes anymore.

My skirt swishes to the ground when I stand, dark spots from lying in the dirt, but it doesn't matter. Nothing matters. I give my skirt a shake though and step back.

My neighborhood is only ten blocks away, not really too far to walk, but I'm not ready. I've already decided that the first time I see it will be the last.

But there's somebody else who needs to see it too.

Chapter Twenty-Nine
Basil

"Do you want to see something interesting?" Nissa rubs at her face, the dark circles under her eyes, worse than usual.

I'm always up for something interesting, and maybe it'll cheer her up. Last night she returned home and wasn't feeling well, so it was the first time we hadn't gotten busy. Her stomach hurt, and she had a fever, so she sent me to the couch so I didn't get sick either.

Breakfast is waiting at the table, and I pour a cup of coffee. She stares at the copper pot in my hand, a faraway expression on her face.

"Of course I am," I say. "Are you okay though? Do you want to rest more?"

She shakes her head and plunks down, her movements mechanical as she takes a bite of the food I made. "We're going to Kjempeland. To see the neighborhood where the house fell from."

The walls close in around me, and I steady myself with a breath. Seeing it again will make it even more real. But maybe I need that, to remind me of the mistakes I've made, to keep me on the path to making things right.

"Sure. But how? I mean, I don't know how to get up there."

"We can take the lyft and walk there." Her voice gets quiet. "I don't know. I thought it might help you to see it."

"It'll be interesting to see what it's like up there. I assume it's double the size as things here."

"I suppose." She shrugs and stares down at her half-full plate. I didn't get a chance to talk to her last night about the drinking, or Mumsy, but we'll have time later today.

We eat a quick breakfast, and I'm about to do dishes, but she tells me we'll get them later. She didn't even make the bed either, so maybe she's planning on coming back and getting more rest.

She grabs her bear, and we head off towards the lyft. I almost tell her I'm going to buy the bear a companion, but she seems to have a lot on her mind, so I stay quiet.

We go into the lyft, a massive box that travels up the side of the white-painted stalk, circling the strand as it slowly rises to the top. People stare at us, but she doesn't notice as she watches out the window.

THE WHOLE STORY

I feel tiny surrounded by these giants. They talk like me, look like me, except they're big. I never gave it much thought, but giants are just like normies, only double sized.

We exit the box, and she takes off down the street.

"You know how to get there?" I ask, taking the surroundings in. The buildings are huge. They're only two or three stories tall, but so much higher than our buildings. I'm a bug here.

"The constable told me. I memorized the directions."

The horses are about the same size as ours, but they pull bigger wagons. We pass a playground with giant swings and slide and continue on. The houses here are as bright as the ones in the neighborhood I'd been in. We could use these colors down below.

Nissa doesn't say much, and a couple times I try reach for her hand, but she shrugs me off. Finally we arrive at the neighborhood I recognize. We pass the house I stole the liquor from and head down the street.

"Wow." I stop. I had pictured what it might look like, but I didn't expect this. There's a huge hole in the ground, and I can see the blue sky of Moorgan below. Their ground isn't actually that thick, and it's different looking from this view compared to by the stalk, where I could hardly see. She tugs me on, and we keep walking.

Soon I can see my neighbor's house and the yard where I once lived.

I did this. I ruined the lives of two families, the giant's and mine. If I could go back, I'd change it in a second, but I can't.

Plastic fencing surrounds the hole. This is where the house was. This is where the three giants who died lived. I know so little about them, only that it was a father, a mother, and a child. I should know their names; I should've asked.

When I get home, I'm going to ask. I need to learn about the people I hurt. It's too late to beg for forgiveness, but I can make sure their memory keeps me on a better path than the one I've been on.

Nissa stares at the gaping hole, a deep sorrow covering her face.

"This is where they lived?" My question is stupid 'cause of course this is the spot. "I don't even know their names."

My face burns with shame. Three people died. Mumsy is going to die. Four deaths will be on my head.

"The father's name was Stein, Mette was his wife, and Giselle was the little girl." Nissa's voice cracks, and I want to sink into the ground and disappear. I've never thought about this family and what was lost.

THE WHOLE STORY

Not Nissa though. For a while I thought she'd been upset 'cause she had a bad experience with giants, but it's not that. She's just a good person. She feels the emotions of others. She cares.

"Are you sorry, Basil?" she asks.

"Sorry for what?" I'm not sure what she's talking about. She gives me a grim smile and pulls back the plastic fencing.

"It's a long way down, isn't it?" Her voice is flat, emotionless.

For half a second I think she's going to jump, and I step over and pull her back.

"Be careful."

"I should've been there," she says, tears filling her eyes.

"Been where. What are you talking about?" The hairs behind my neck prickle up.

"I have something for you." She reaches into her bag with her free hand, the bear clutched in the other, but I'm not sure I want to see what she has. She pulls out the pink polka dot brassiere I stole from the house behind me and holds it up in front of her.

I can't breathe. *Think, think, think.*

"I found it in the debris. I know it was dumb of me, but I was fascinated by it. I shouldn't have kept it."

She must have found it in the woods. I shouldn't have held onto it.

"Did you? It fell from the sky?"

"Yes. You've got to believe me. I'll throw it away. I shouldn't have kept it."

She snorted. "You're still lying to me. You don't care about anyone but yourself."

"No, that's not true. I love you." The words surprise me, but they're true. I don't want to be with any other woman. "You've changed my life."

"And you changed mine," she says, wiping her eyes again.

Chapter Thirty
Nissa

Basil is a liar. He's never told me the truth, not once. Not about what he did, not about his Mumsy, not about anything.

I can't take the pain inside me. I miss my parents and Giselle so much; I just want this to be over. I want him out of my life.

I'm not sure I can do this though. It's so hard, but I can't stop now. I take a deep breath and steady my voice.

"You need to come clean, Basil." I pull the plastic case with the coins out of my bag. Special coins my pop got for me and Giselle.

He gasps when I hold the case up. "Do you see this?" I flip the case over to the backside to show the letters on the back.

N and G

"Do you know what this means?" I ask. He shakes his head, his eyes wide and his lips in a tight line. There's fear there, something I'm seeing for the first time in his eyes. "It means Nissa and Giselle. My father bought them when he was on a trip once. He brought them home for me and my sister, and we kept them in a tin can with a bunch of other coins."

"No." His face pales, and he backs away from me, repeating the no. "Oh god, I'm sorry." His voice trembles, the shock in his eyes. He's finally feeling a small part of the agony I live with every day. He'll never feel what I feel though.

"I didn't mean for anything to happen," he babbles. "I just… I was just trying to… I didn't want anyone to die. I—"

I drop the coins to the ground and hold up my hand. "Stop," I yell. "Do you care about anyone but yourself?"

"I love you. You've got to believe me. I'd change it all if I could." He drops to his knees and clasps his hands. "Please forgive me."

I don't care anymore. I'm done. I just want to be with the people who love me.

"Goodbye, Basil." I clutch Giselle's bear to my chest, step to the edge of the hole and off into nothingness.

I'm falling, the screams of Basil following me down. I can see him peering over the edge, reaching for me, but I'm too far away.

THE WHOLE STORY

The joy fills me because very soon I'll be with my parents and sister again. I'll be at peace. And that's the only place I want to be.

"Goodbye," I whisper.

And then I am no more.

The End

Acknowledgments

Thank you to Theresa Paolo, for helping me shape this story and offering advice in so many other ways.

Thank you also to my writer friends who are always there for advice and help.

And mostly, thanks to you, the person who has picked up this story to read. These fairy tale retellings in my Down the Twisted Path series are a little different compared to my other writing, but they've been fun to work on. And I have more coming.

About the Author

Reading has always been a big part of Suzi's life. She even won the most-pages-read award a few times in her junior high English class, many years ago. She started several writing projects as a kid but never actually finished anything, and then she took a big break from writing that lasted well into adulthood.

She writes in a variety of genres, including horror, suspense, and women's fiction, and she has even dipped into fantasy slightly with her fairy tale retellings. She also writes young adult novels under the name Suzi Drew.

Her non-writing life includes her family and friends, her sweet and fluffy dog, and an awesome job editing with CookieLynn Publishing. (Oh wait, that's still a part of writing. Seems she can't get away from the written word!)

To find out more about Suzi,
go to SuziWieland.com

Also by Suzi Wieland

Thriller Novels
Black Diamond Dogs

Horror Novels
House of Desire

Horror and Suspense Novellas/Short Stories
Shallow Depths
(Un)lucky Thirteen
Long-Term Effects
The Silent Treatment
A Story to Tell
Panne Dora Pass

Twisted Twins Series
Glenda and Gus
Two for the Price of One
A Hard Split

Fairy Tale Novellas
The Down the Twisted Path Series
The Whole Story
An Unwanted Life
Killing Rosie
The Perfect Meal
When the Forest Cries
In the Queen's Dark Light

Please visit SuziWieland.com
for more information.

Milton Keynes UK
Ingram Content Group UK Ltd.
UKHW031155251124
451529UK00001B/14